FROM THE KIWI KINGDOM SERIES

THE RISE OF KORU

Rosemary Thomas, the author of nine titles in the Kiwi Kingdom Series, was born and brought up on New Zealand's West Coast in Westland; where the Kiwi Kingdom is set.   Rosemary is a retired Nurse, Mother and Grandmother. Living with her husband in Western Australia, walks in nature, making craft for charity and writing fill her days.

Her mother's love of writing began in the 2000's. Writing prose about places Rosemary visited was the beginning of her venture into writing. A dream of Keanu and Keona's journey to Lake Kaniere resulted in "The Kiwi Kingdom" being published in 2010. By then, a prequel – Keoni's Kingdom, and sequel – Kupe Kiwi's Kingdom were waiting to be written. They are now incorporated into "Under the Blowholes Spray." Kohana's Quest, Koa's Kingdom and Odelia's Challenge have been incorporated into "The Islands."

For June
Much Love
Rosemary xx 2022

BY ROSEMARY THOMAS

In the Kiwi Kingdom series:

Under the Blowholes Spray
- Keoni's Kingdom
- Return of the Kiwi Kingdom (The Kiwi Kingdom)
- Kupe Kiwi's Kingdom

The Islands
- Kohana's Quest
- Koa's Kingdom
- Odelia's Challenge

The Driftwood Shore

Beneath the Long White Cloud

The Rise of Koru

Also

CAPTIVES

The Kiwi Kingdom is also on Facebook.

Information about the publishing of titles by the Author can be found on this page. Organisations that care for Kiwi and other animals in the real Kiwi Kingdom are also promoted on this page.

ISBN: 97806487406-5-0   Paperback edition

ABN: 61517596692

The Rise of Koru by Rosemary Thomas

All the events in the book and the characters in them are pure fiction. Any similarities to real people, living or dead, are a coincidence and not intended by the Author.

Front Cover photograph by the Author.

Printed and bound in Australia by Ingram Spark, First Printing April 2022

Contact for Author: rosemarythomas19@hotmail.com

THE RISE OF KORU

From the Kiwi Kingdom Series

The Rise of Koru

THE LONG WAY HOME

Kita the Roroa Kiwi stretched, as he emerged from the temporary burrow he shared with Kimo and Kohu. It had been a long journey, since they had fled from the threats they had received from Kahine Kiwi, at their own community in the Buller. Kahine had considered them a threat to be eliminated. Hopefully they would be welcomed in the Tasman.

Kita sensed that he was being watched. Looking up, he saw a Morepork Owl/Ruru sitting watching him.

"Hello." Kita called softly. Kimo and Kohu were still asleep. He didn't want to wake them just yet, as he liked to have some time alone, on this long journey to their new home.

"Are you from Kerwin's community?"

"I am." The Ruru confirmed. "Stay here. Kerwin is coming to meet you."

Kita thought it was a strange request, but didn't question it. "We will."

As the Ruru left the area to tell Kerwin they were waiting for him, Kita started to feed in the surrounding bush, which was full of dense ferns, beneath the moss covered tree trunks. A rustle from the burrow told Kita that Kimo and Kohu were up.

"Are you ready to go?" Kohu asked when Kita appeared.

"We are to stay put." Kita replied. "I was told by a Ruru from Kerwin's community that Kerwin is coming to meet us."

"Did it say why?" Kimo asked with concern.

"No." Kita allowed himself to show his worry. "I think we may need a plan B."

"You mean we aren't wanted here?"

Kita nodded. "We should be prepared for that. We don't know how things are in this community. They may feel threatened by three new strange males competing for the available females."

"What will we do?" Kohu asked. "We can't go back to the Buller."

"I agree." Kita looked over towards the Kaikoura Range. "If we are asked to leave, then we will head over to the east and make our way down to the Alps and Arthurs Pass. I know the communities down there are always happy for new members to join them. Shall we have a feed while we are waiting for Kerwin to come?"

Kohu looked around. He sensed that Kerwin wouldn't be alone. "I think it would be best if Kimo and I move over by that big tree." He indicated a large Totara tree some distance to the south.

"If anything happens, we can just slip away."

Just then, the Ruru returned. He saw Kohu and Kimo leave. "You should join them if you want to stay safe."

"Thanks." Kita replied, before swiftly joining Kohu and Kimo to flee from the area.

When Kerwin reached the tree where the Ruru was waiting, he was half relieved to find no sign of Kita and his friends.

"Are they hiding?" Kerwin asked the Ruru. Males from his community had surrounded the tree.

"No. they have gone back home. They guessed that they weren't welcome here and left."

Kerwin nodded. "See! Your problem is already solved." Kerwin addressed the males that were with him. Some weren't convinced.

"Shouldn't we follow them and make sure they can't come back?"

"There's no need!" Kerwin's tone was firm. "Would you hang around a place where you found that you weren't welcome and could be killed? Remember, they came here for sanctuary, not to conquer! Come along! We have classes to attend." With that, Kerwin turned and led the way back to the community.

When Kita and his friends eventually stopped running, they hid under a large log and listened. They were greeted with silence. Tentatively, they moved out to have a feed before moving on. Kita sensed something land in the branch above them. It was the Ruru he had seen.

"Are they coming?" Kita asked in alarm, preparing to flee.

"No, you are safe." The Ruru reassured him. "They have gone back to the community. Where are you heading now?

"We aren't safe at Buller, so we are heading for the Alps. The communities at Arthurs Pass welcome new members."

"We will let them know you are coming." The Ruru smiled. From then on, Kita noticed that Ruru seemed to be nearby at all times, keeping an eye on their progress.   Back at the Tasman community, Kerwin was being challenged.

"Are you sure those Kiwis have gone and aren't sneaking around here?"

"Yes! I am sure they aren't sneaking around here!" Kerwin couldn't help showing his impatience. " I have the Ruru following them. They are well south of here and are heading to the Arthurs Pass Community in the Alps. They know they will be welcome there."

With this knowledge, the males in the Tasman community finally settled down to their usual domestic squabbling.

The incident however, left Kerwin unsettled. It had taken a lot more reassurance than usual, to convince the Kiwis in his community that he had managed the situation how they wanted. He was now wondering just how safe he was in this community. Remembering how ruthless they had been during the war, when the previous leader had attempted to take over communities to the south, Kerwin knew there would be little mercy or chance of escape, if they decided to turn against him. Kerwin now was hypervigilant to the atmosphere around him. He also realised that someone was usually watching him! Kerwin started to consider an exit from here, but the only safe way was north! There was his mate to consider too! Would she come with him if he left and what about his children? He knew they would be eliminated if they stayed behind.

In the long months that lay ahead, Kita and his friends made their way south, through the dense forest and the many streams in their path. When they arrived at the Buller River, They had to travel west to find a suitable ford over the river. As the three very damp Kiwis made their way out the other side, they were being watched. With sad eyes, Kerewa watched them disappear into the forest.

So, Kita and his friends attempt to live in Kerwin's community hadn't been successful after all. He just wished them luck with their lives in the south. He hadn't heard from Kerwin for a while and wondered whether all was well up there.

Kita Kohu and Kimo were relieved when they sighted the Southern Alps ahead of them. They were almost home! On a very wet night as they made their up the Otira Gorge, Kita saw movement ahead. He made a soft call. Kita's call was answered by a very loud one!

"WELCOME HOME!"

It was Koen, the Roroa leader at Arthurs Pass. With a beaming smile he led them to the community that were waiting to welcome them.

"How are things up in the Buller?" Koen wanted to know. He had been told that Kita and his friends were coming to live with them, but not much else.

"When we left, Kerewa's son Kahine was threatening to kill us, as he won't share power when he becomes leader. We went up to Kerwin's community in the Tasman. But, as we approached their community, we were asked to wait for him to meet us. We thought this was suspicious, so Kohu and Kimo retreated to a safe distance. A Ruru told me it wasn't safe for me to stay, so we all fled. We've been making our way down here since."

Koen sent a message to the Buller to let Kailan

know that Kita and his friends had arrived safely. He was alarmed to hear that Kahine had been expelled from the community, to the Alps, but had headed to Three Sisters Community to attack Kotare. Kailan had followed Kahine, only for them both to die from their injuries when they met in their battle.

KARI

At the Buller community, Kerewa was also nervous! Everyone had taken the joint leadership by both Kerewa and Kailan, for granted, but now that only Kerewa remained, he had to be extra careful to make decisions that suited everyone. After seeing Kita and his friends cross the Buller River, Kerewa now knew that there was no chance of Kita returning to represent his family. He decided to go and see Kari, who was still grieving from the loss of Kailan. After asking how she was, Kerewa came to the point.

"I would like you take Kailan's place as leader."

Kari looked at Kerewa with incredulous eyes!

"But I'm a ……

"female." Kerewa finished for her. He smiled.

"I expect you will do fine! Remember that my second mother Kohana, was leader of the whole kingdom! Kailan will be proud of you!"

"Very well then. What happens now?"

"We will tell everyone the good news! I will meet you at the meeting area." With that, Kerewa put out a call for everyone to attend the meeting area.

Kari had been in the depths of despair at the loss of Kailan and also their son Kita who was now in the north, and not expected to return. She now had a purpose to her life – to represent Kailan's family and supporters. She also realised that she need not take another male as protection, as she would be in the role of protector. If she was to take another male to produce more children, it would be her, who would be doing the choosing!

Kari took her time to make her way to the meeting, revelling in the power her new position gave her. She was almost the last to arrive. The Kari that took her place next to Kerewa was a very different Kari to the one that everyone had grown to know in bereavement. This Kari strode in with purpose, her head held high and with a gleam in her eyes.

"Thank you all for coming." Kerewa began with a big smile. He along with everyone else was astonished at the transformation of Kari. "I have invited Kari to represent Kailan and his family as co-leader of our community. Are there any objections?" His question was met with silence.

"That's settled then."

As everyone crowded around Kari to congratulate her, there were a few downcast male members among the crowd. They had expected some competition among themselves to be Kari's next partner. Also, they had expected to be the dominant partner in the relationship with her. Most important of all, they had expected to have an influence in the future running of the community. It was obvious to everyone, that this Kari wasn't going to tolerate being dominated by anyone! And she certainly wasn't interested in sharing the power she now had in representing her family in the community. There was only one glimmer of hope for them, was she pregnant? She would be needing a partner to help her hatch her chick.

The question of who would help hatch Kari's egg was already occupying her mind, adding to her depressed state. Ever since Kailan had been taken from her, she had been dreading the day when she would be expected to take another male for her partner.

Kari went to feed before settling in her burrow. Predawn light was beginning to lighten the Buller Valley when a shadow came across the opening to her home.

"Kari, are you there?"

"Come in." Kari recognised one of the females, Kota who had also been left without a partner. She thought Kota had found another partner, so wondered what she wanted.

"I'm wondering whether you can help me." Kota began. "I thought my new partner would help me with the chick I am carrying, but he is only interested in hatching his own. He wants me to discard this one!" The despair in her voice told Kari that Kota still cared for her chick, just as she needed to protect Kailan's legacy.

"We can help each other!" Kari smiled at Kota. "I have a chick to protect too!

Kota came to live with Kari in her burrow, to the disappointment of the available males in the community. They would have to look for other opportunities now.

Kerewa's partner Katana came to see how they were getting on together, and was amazed at how contented both Kari and Kota looked.

"You both are looking very well!" Katana commented. "You aren't missing having a male with you?"

Kari just smiled, but Kota made her feelings clear!

"My new male wanted me to discard my egg!

Would you put up with having your son or daughter destroyed Katana?"

Katana was silent for a few moments as she digested this news.

"No I wouldn't!" Katana agreed. "Let me know if you need any help." Silently hoping that she would never be put in the position of having to protect the life of her chick the way Kari and Kota were having to do.

"Are there any other mothers in the community, like you too?" Katana asked. "Perhaps we can help them too."

"That's a great idea!" Both Kari and Kota were enthusiastic. "Between us we can talk to all the females in the community and let it be known they can come to us for help."

In the coming nights, it became clear that help was indeed needed for their females. Four were paired together, much to their relief. Another female who had recently taken another male broke down and cried as she had already discarded her egg to begin again. She was happy to know she would never have to do it again.

Some of the males weren't happy that the available females were suddenly living with other females and not interested in them anymore, complained to Kerewa. He mentioned the fact to Katana.

"It's hardly surprising!" Katana replied with some spirit, which surprised Kerewa, as he wasn't used to Katana being so assertive. "Many of the males expect their new females to discard the eggs they are carrying if they belong to another male." Katana looked at Kerewa. "How would you feel if something happened to you and

I was forced to discard our son or daughter? Katana rubbed her expanding tummy as she spoke.

"I wouldn't be happy." Kerewa admitted.

"You can tell the males that complained, that they need to be patient. The females are living together to protect their chicks. They should be available after their children are hatched and are independent."

There was a certain amount of grumbling, but acceptance of the new situation, where the females supported each other. Some Kiwis doubted the wisdom of having a female in charge. How could she protect them?

Their question was answered one moonless night. The sound of a dog and humans approaching in the distance with spotlights. Most Kiwis fled to their burrows in fear, remembering the last time, when Kohana Kiwi arranged for the community to cross the river to safety while she stayed to find Kelia. Kohana's bravery in protecting Kelia from the dog, cost her, her life.

Kari knew what she had to do! – and it didn't include cowering in her burrow! She hid behind a tree while the dog passed her. Kari then ran out from the tree and jumped onto the dog's back, raking it with her sharp claws and pecking its head furiously with her bill. She managed to strike the dog in its eye. The dog yelped and howled as it desperately shook itself to rid it of the torment from the creature.

It was only when the dog sat down, that Kari slid off its back. By now the men had Kari and the dog in their spotlights. Kari gave the dog a swipe on the nose which sent it running away towards the river. Despite the searing light in her eyes, Kari now directed her attention to the men and charged at them, ready to rake their legs!

"S*@#t! We had better get out of here!" The Men then turned tail, whistling for the dog to come. Kari kept hard on their heels until she was satisfied they wouldn't be staying around. Once the sound of the men and the dog had retreated into the distance. Kari then put out a call to say it was now safe, before retreating to her burrow for a rest.

"Oh Kari!" Kota cried with relief when Kari entered their burrow. "Are you alright?"

"I'm fine." Kari replied, though she was now shaking like a leaf, not only from the adrenaline still coursing through her body, but also from the realisation that her encounter with the dog and humans could have ended very differently.

"I will go and get us something to eat." Kota slipped out of the burrow to find everyone crowding around.

"Is she alright?" came the chorus from the crowd.

"Kari will be fine. She is just calming down."

"Are you sure?" Katana asked with concern.

"Yes. She hasn't been harmed at all."

Kerewa came to the burrow entrance. "Kari, We all want to thank you for being so brave and protecting us." He turned to the crowd. "We will leave her in peace to recover." Before leading them all away.

When Kota returned with some worms for Kari, Katana brought some for her as well. Kota was relieved to see Kari had stopped shaking and appeared much calmer. She accepted the worms with relish, realising how hungry she was. Kari also realised with pride that she had now proven herself in her role as leader, to protect the community.

KERWIN & KARAMU'S ESCAPE

Kerwin looked around carefully before moving swiftly out of his burrow. It was broad daylight, but pouring rain was beating down. He was glad that the rain prevented anyone from hearing him, as he moved around. Looking behind him, Kerwin's two children, Kahuia his daughter and Kamahi his son were following close behind.

They headed north, towards the waterfall. Kerwin had already said goodbye to his mate, Karamu. She had refused to consider leaving. She had been here all her life, even if staying meant risking her life. Karamu could not believe that the males would kill an available female. She wasn't sure whether she was carrying Kerwin's child. At the worst, she would have to abandon the egg after she delivered it.

Karamu wanted to stay for another reason - to keep the school going. Kerwin had been taking the classes, which attracted animals from near and far. She didn't want to imagine the community returning to its previous practice, of being completely separate to all the animals around them. With this in mind, Karamu curled herself up with her back to the entrance, to return to sleep.

Karamu's attempt to sleep was rudely interrupted by a sharp claw that was shaking her. She turned her head to see one of the females standing over her.

"Where have your family gone, and why are you still here?"

Karamu ignored the question about her family.

"I am staying to keep the school going. I will probably be mated with someone else."

"If you stay, the males will kill you! If they don't kill you, I will! Your mate and your family is more important than the school!"

There was no mistaking the fury on the face of the female.

Karamu turned and headed towards the entrance. She hesitated for a second deciding which way to go, luckily it was still raining, but found herself propelled out of her burrow by the big claws of the female. Karamu crashed through the bushes as she ran for her life. If the community wasn't awake before, they should be now! She found herself heading for the coast. Karamu had no idea how long she ran for, not looking back, or stopping to see if she was being followed. When she could run no further, Karamu hid behind a tree, as she tried to get her breath back. She could hear the ocean in the distance. Once Karamu was sure she hadn't been followed, she kept walking towards the ocean, heading south at the same time; stopping to feed as she went. Coming across a wide track - she knew it was made by humans, Karamu followed it, knowing it would lead her to somewhere. When dusk came she made a temporary burrow, lapsing into a dreamless sleep.

Kerwin led Kahuia and Kamahi to the side of the waterfall. He knew of a cave behind the flowing water, where they could shelter. Kerwin's plan was dashed, when he saw the entrance was full of water. Silently he led them up the steep fern covered bank to the top, to follow the stream inland. They too fed as they travelled, stopping to sleep in a temporary burrow once it became dark.

In the Tasman community, there was fury from those who had intended to eliminate Kerwin, when they were ready to take over. There was also fear among those who had been happy with Kerwin's leadership. While no-one had seen Kerwin and his children leave, some members had seen Karamu flee for her life. They kept their knowledge to themselves.

Volunteers were asked for to search for the family, and to eliminate them when they found them.

"How far south do you want us to go?" the question was asked. "Kerewa and Kailan will protect them if they reach that far."

"Just go after them. They can't have gone that far."

Some of the volunteers were supporters of Kerwin. They had no intention of returning. They also were going to make sure the rebels' supporters weren't returning either. During that night, a number of families also slipped away into the darkness. The rebels found that only a quarter of the community now remained with them.

Kerwin and his children emerged from their burrow. They had a couple of hours before daylight to feed and continue on their journey south. As they started to forage, Kerwin though he heard a noise nearby. Quickly he herded the children behind a tree.

"Kerwin?" a soft call came from the other side of the tree.

Cautiously, Kerwin put his head around the tree. A couple of families stood there, grins on their faces.

"You've got company. Have you seen Karamu yet?"

"No. When did she leave?"

"In the daytime. She was seen running for her life. We think she headed for the coast." The kiwi paused. "We will have to be careful. The rebels sent a party to search for you, though some of your supporters are among them."

Kerwin nodded as he digested this news. He had been mourning the fact that he wouldn't see Karamu again. Now there was a chance, if the search party didn't find her first.

Karamu came out of her burrow. The only animal sounds she could hear, was of some ruru calling nearby. She was making her way south, when the sound of rapid footsteps made her pause. To her horror, it was one of the rebel supporters coming straight for her! Karamu put up her claw to defend herself, only to watch in amazement as two kiwis came rushing to tackle him. A brief furious fight left him lifeless on the floor.

"Where are you heading?" the two kiwis asked Karamu with a grin.

"Down to Kerewa and Kailan's community at the Buller. Hopefully I will meet Kerwin there."

"Allow us to give you an escort."

As Karamu smiled her acceptance and relief, the kiwi put out a call. Another two kiwis appeared from the dense forest to join them.

During the coming nights, more families joined

with both Kerwin and Karamu as they headed south.

The first Kerewa heard of the coming community, was when a message came from the Ruru in the Tasman area.

'Kerwin, his children and a number of families from the Tasman community were now heading south. Karamu his mate also was heading south with some families, on a separate path down the coast.'

Kerewa sent the message. 'How many are left up there?'

'Very few.'

Kerewa knew he had to call a meeting, to at least prepare for their arrival, even if the community's stay was only temporary. He put out a call for everyone to attend the meeting area.

Kari swiftly moved her egg to Kota to care for, before seeking out Kerewa.

"What is the problem?" Kari asked.

"Kerwin and most of his community in the Tasman are coming. We need to prepare for their arrival, whether this community allows them to stay or move on."

"Should we allow them to stay?"

"Wherever they settle, Kerwin won't have a leadership role, unless they start a new community of their own."

"I agree." Kari replied, before returning to sit on her egg. Kiwis heading to the meeting area saw them conferring and wondered what was happening, especially when Kari didn't attend the meeting.

"We have heard," Kerewa informed the

community, "that Kerwin and most of his community are heading our way. We need to prepare for their arrival, regardless of whether you allow them to stay or move elsewhere."

"What if they stay? Are we having another leader here?" the question was asked.

"Kari and I have agreed. Kerwin won't have a leadership role here. They will have to start their own community elsewhere for him to be in charge."

"They will be moving on then?"

"We will put it to a vote, and remember we will still be welcoming them and allowing them to stay while they decide where their future home will be."

At the end of the meeting, everyone went off to prepare some temporary burrows for the new arrivals.

Kerewa and Katana were out feeding, when Opal came to sit on a nearby branch.

"Kerwin and his community will be here soon."

"Can you go and lead them in?" Kerewa asked Opal.

Opal nodded and sped off, wondering how the latest arrivals would be received here. It had been obvious at the meeting that they wouldn't be encouraged to stay.

As Kerwin approached the Buller Community, with Opal leading the way, he was both relieved and anxious. Relieved that he was safe at last, but also anxious how he and his community would be received here. Kerwin already accepted that he wouldn't have a leadership role if they were able to stay. He also knew that he needed a plan B if they were told to move on. He also wondered whether his mate Karamu had arrived yet.

Kerwin had already tried to prepare the families for the fact that their stay here may be temporary.

"Surely they wouldn't kick us out!?" were the comments when Kerwin brought up the subject.

Kerwin reminded them of the fact, the previous leader of their community Kaine, had waged war on their neighbouring community, with intentions of taking over this one too! The community here hadn't forgotten that their leader Kehi, had given his life to end the conflict. They were not to get too comfortable, as he would be looking for another place for them to set up their own community. With that promise, they had to be satisfied.

When Kerwin and the now weary families approached Kerewa and Kari, the community was also there too. Kerwin and the families noticed there weren't any smiles of welcome, which confirmed their fear, that they weren't welcome here.

"Thank you for welcoming us." Kerwin began. "Our stay will only be temporary while I find a suitable site for us to make our permanent home." Kerwin saw visible signs of relief on the faces of the community here, when he stated they weren't intending to stay. "Has Karamu and the families she is bringing, arrived yet?"

"Not yet." Kerewa replied, "But their progress is being monitored. They should be here in a couple of nights. Our community has made some temporary burrows for you. You will be shown to your burrows and feeding areas too, before you settle for your rest time. There will be a meeting to tell you about your future home when it is decided."

Kari turned and nodded to their community members who had volunteered to welcome the new arrivals. They came forward to take each family to their burrow and show them where to feed. Other community members melted into the forest to continue their routine.

Kerewa showed Kerwin and his children their burrow and took them for a feed, asking Kerwin what happened to split up their community.

Kerwin told him that it was usual for his community to squabble a lot, and all seemed normal until word came of Kita and his friends journey to them. The community made it clear, they were suspicious, and wanted to eliminate them. Kerwin knew he had to protect Kita and his friends, so he sent a local Ruru to warn them. The community would have killed them, if they had stayed to meet him.

Then Kerwin a realised that he was also under constant surveillance, that he was at risk now too. Kerwin had tried to persuade Karamu to come with him and their children, but she didn't want to leave the place she had lived all her life. He had heard since that Karamu also had to flee.

"I understand what you have been through, and the pressures you still have." Kerewa's tone was sympathetic. "Dad suffered the same surveillance when he was leader here, only it was our mother that was killed. He would have been next, but there was a confrontation that sorted the issue."

"What happened to those plotting against him?"

"They were all killed."

Kerewa looked at Kerwin with interest. "It looks like your community have voted with their feet." At Kerwin's enquiring look, he explained. "Most of your community have elected to come with you. You must have done something right while you were in charge there."

Just then, a couple of young kiwis from the local community came up to Kahuia and Kamahi, asking whether they would like to join them at their school. Kahuia and Kamahi's eyes lit up, but looked at their father for his approval first.

Kerewa smiled. "Yes, you can join them."

Other juveniles from Kerwin's community also came to see what was happening. The school teacher had a much larger class that night.

"Your school was a success up there, then." Kerewa commented.

"It was. I'm sorry I had to leave it. I expect the school will be destroyed now we are gone." A look of determination came over Kerwin. "I will be starting another one when we get settled. Do you have an atlas among your books? I want to start looking for a suitable site for us to live."

"Of course we have an atlas!" Kerewa reassured Kerwin. "When the school session is finished, I will take you to have a look. Depending which community will be the closest, we will organise some more books for you."

Karamu and her group were now making their way inland, among the many hills and streams in their path towards the Buller community. A Ruru was shadowing their journey. They had been told that

Kerwin and his group had arrived there. Karamu would be glad when this journey was over. In a couple of weeks she would need to nest.

Kerewa had the atlas open at the South Island, and was showing Kerwin where all the other communities now lived.

"We are here." Kerewa indicated the north side of the Buller River.

"Kuaka's community is here." indicating The Three Sisters Mountain, in the Paparoa range.

"One place you could settle, is the Ohikanui Valley." Kerewa suggested. "It is long, with a river running through it. No humans are near it. It isn't far to either our community or Kuaka, if you needed help.

"Kanoa's community is here." indicating the Paparoa Range south of Three Sister's Mountain. "Kanoa has passed to the spirit world now. His son Kamoku is living at Three Sisters Mountain at present.

'Koen's community is at Arthur's Pass and Koa is with the community in the Arahura valley."

Kerwin smiled at the mention of Koa.

"How is Koa?" Kerwin wanted to know. He had missed his friend while in the north.

"Koa has a family he is bring up too."

"Lake Kaniere has a school, but no Kiwis are there now. The last I heard; Spirit harriers were causing trouble there. Humans live down by the lake shore too." He pointed at the map. "We have a Rowi community, but they are at Okarito; and a Tokoeka community at Fiordland. Down the south you have to consider that both the wet and snow affects breeding and feeding."

24

"The community won't thank me for taking them into the Alps in the Winter months. It looks like the Ohikanui Valley is the best place for us." Kerwin paused, "or Lake Kaniere." Kerwin grinned at Kerewa.

"It sounds like they need some help at Kaniere!" When Karamu and her group arrive, we will have a meeting to decide. We are coming up to breeding season, so Ohikanui may be the best place untill all the chicks are independent. If they like it there, we will stay, if not, we will move down to Kaniere."

"That sounds like a sensible plan." Kerewa voiced his approval.

When Kerwin returned to his burrow, some of his community were anxiously waiting for him.

"Have you found a place for us?" they wanted to know.

"I have found a couple of places that may be suitable." Kerwin reassured them. "We are just waiting now for Karamu's group to arrive. We will have a meeting then to decide."

"That's a couple of nights away, isn't it?" one asked. "We may not be able to wait till then."

"You have been threatened?" Kerwin's voice was quiet.

The kiwi nodded miserably. Kerwin looked around. He was sure their conversation would be monitored.

"Come into my burrow. Someone keep guard."

Kerwin told them of the valley on the other side of the river, which was intended as a temporary home, to see whether they liked it or not.

"Can we go tonight?"

"You can. It would be best for you to walk upstream to the bridge, then come back to the valley. I will show you where the valley is. The Buller river has strong currents. I don't want you to risk drowning!"

When Kerwin came outside, his community was waiting. Silently, he led them to the river, where the bridge over the Ohikanui was visible.

"Our new home is over there, beyond that bridge. We have to walk upstream to a bridge to cross the river, then come back."

As the community set out, Kerewa came running up.

"What's going on?"

Kerwin kept his voice calm as he answered.

"Some of our members have reported that they have been threatened. We are choosing to move to our new home tonight. I am relying on you to control your community while we remove ourselves from your area." Kerwin paused before continuing in a steely tone. "If we are attacked, I will not be responsible if our members harm or kill them!"

"Once our community is safe in our valley, I will be returning to meet Karamu's group. Can you send one of your Ruru to lead me to them; avoiding your territory of course."

"There is no need..." Kerewa began.

"Yes there is!" Kerwin insisted. "I know you personally won't harm me or my community, but we can't trust your community."

"I will walk with you." Kerewa offered.

Kerwin agreed. Both Kerewa and Kerwin, along with his Community could feel many eyes on them as they made their way to the bridge. Thanks to Kerewa's presence, their journey was uneventful.

"Where are the boundaries of your territory?" Kerwin wanted to know.

When Kerewa showed him, Kerwin was relieved to find that the area by the bridge was outside it. On the other side of the river, a Ruru came to join Kerwin as he led his community.

"I'm Opal. I am here to escort you."

"Thanks Opal."

There was much relief, when the community crossed the bridge over the Ohikanui river and started to make their way into the valley.

"Go beyond that bluff," Kerwin advised them. "and make yourselves comfortable. I have to go back and find Karamu's group and make sure they get here safely."

"You want someone to come with you?" came offers from concerned kiwis.

"No. Opal will keep me safe."

While the community slowly made their way along the valley floor, exploring their new home, Kerwin swiftly returned to the bridge to confer with Opal.

"How far is Karamu and her group from Kerewa's community?" Kerwin wanted to know.

"Not far." Opal admitted.

"Is there a narrow part of the river I can cross, that will bring me closer to them quickly?"

"You can swim well?" Opal was doubtful.

"I can!" Kerwin reassured her.

Keeping low, Opal led Kerwin downstream to a steep bank. The river narrowed here, with a wide shingle bank on the other side.

"You will be swept down the river." Opal advised Kerwin. "Just go with it as you go across."

Kerwin headed her advice as he struck out, letting the current carry him. Before he knew it, he was touching the bottom on the other side. Kerwin scrambled out to rush into the cover of the surrounding bushland, with Opal following behind him.

"How far away are they?" Kerwin asked.

"You have time to reach them and take them to the valley before morning. You will have to travel the long way round to reach the bridge."

"I agree. I can't see them swimming the river against the current."

Karamu was looking forward to reaching the Buller community. They expected to be there the next night. As her group steadily made their way through the forest, a Ruru called in the distance. The Ruru who had been shadowing them answered.

"What's happening?" Karamu asked the Ruru.

"Kerwin is coming."

Karamu called the group to her. "Kerwin is meeting us!" As they waited, a Ruru approached from the river. Behind them, a lone figure was running towards them.

Karamu found she was swept into Kerwin's embrace.

"I'm so happy you are safe!"

28

"How far is it to the Buller community?" Kerwin was asked.

"We aren't going to that community. We are going to our new home instead. We will be there before morning."

The serious tone of Kerwin's voice, told them that there was a problem with the Buller community. It was confirmed when Kerwin asked Opal a question.

"Opal, how close will we be passing to the community?"

"Too close!"

Kerwin advised the group. "From now on, we need to be silent, until we have crossed the river."

With Opal leading, and the other Ruru following the group, they made their way past the Buller territory as fast as they could, making sure the children weren't left behind. They were safely across the bridge, before they took the time to feed and relax a little.

In the Ohikanui valley, Kerwin led them towards the bluff.

"Who's there?" came the challenge.

"Just Kerwin." He replied with a smile.

"And the rest of us!" A kiwi in the group added.

"So you made it! Welcome home!"

Kerwin and the group found themselves surrounded by the families who had found a suitable area up on the hillside for their burrows, above the flood line.

Predawn light was filtering through the trees when Kerwin started digging to make their burrow.

"What are you doing Kerwin? Your burrow is

over here!" Kerwin looked around with amazement. Kiwis he had left to set up their homes were offering him one that was done. He hadn't expected it, after the night they had gone through.

"It's our thanks for saving us all."

Karamu had taken Kahuia and Kamahi with her to gather some ferns to make their home comfortable. They would be wanting their own separate tunnels, but there was plenty of time for that.

As the Bellbirds led the dawn chorus across the valley, Kerwin and Karamu finally cuddled up together, secure that they and their community were safe. His one regret at leaving the north, was the loss of the school that he had established there.

NEW SCHOOL IN THE NORTH

Oreana the Ruru heard the sound of fleeing feet above the rain beating outside their nesting hollow. She swiftly put her head out to see the backs of Kerwin and his children, Kahuia and Kamahi. There was no sign of Kerwin's mate Karamu. Even though it was daylight, she needed to know what was happening.

She put out a silent call to Kohana, before turning to look at her mate Oren, who was now awake, and looking at her anxiously.

"What's up?"

"Something drastic has happened at the Kiwi community. I have just seen Kerwin and his children fleeing during their sleep time. There is no sign of his mate. I have called Kohana."

I'm here! Kohana's voice came from behind her. Oreana looked behind her to see Kohana and Titan now in the hollow with her.

"They are here. Hopefully I won't be long."

Can you take me to the Kiwi community? Kerwin and his children have just fled. There is no sign of his mate. We need to protect the books at the school if we can.

Kohana grabbed Oreana's claw before they disappeared from view. First, they visited Kerwin's burrow, where they could see Karamu curled up inside. They were about to leave when a large female Kiwi came to shake Karamu awake. They could hear her threaten to kill Karamu, before forcing her out of the burrow.

Karamu also fled, towards the coast. They followed the female back to her burrow, before Oreana showed Kohana where the school cave was.

We need to find somewhere safe for these books, before the kiwis wake up. Now that Kerwin is gone, they will probably destroy them.

There is a dry hollow near your nesting tree we could store them untill you find another place for your classes. Kohana suggested. Oreana agreed.

It took time, but with Titan's help they took all but one book to safety.

We will see what they do here tonight! Was Kohana's comment as she returned Oreana to Oren.

"Karamu has had to flee too!" Oreana told Oren as she snuggled up with him. "We have saved most of the books, so I can restart classes."

"Why didn't you save all of them?" Oren was puzzled.

"We want to see whether it is only Kerwin they want to remove, or whether they want to stop the classes too. If they destroy the book we left behind, we will know that we will have to find another place well away from this community for our school."

Oreana joined the other Ruru as they took their young to the school that night. They sat on a nearby tree branch to watch the chaotic scene below. Several kiwis were chasing away any animal, including kiwis who tried to enter the school cave.

"It's over! There is no more school here!" they were shouting. There were sounds of destruction inside.

"It's just as well the books are safe!" Oreana made the comment.

"They are?" The Ruru were looking at Oreana with amazement.

Oreana nodded. "We need to find another safe place for classes, well away from this community."

It took the knowledge of some bats to find their new school. In a remote valley, where no kiwis ventured, there was a system of caves. One of them was dry.

The rebel kiwis had been puzzled to find only one book remaining in the cave. They had searched everywhere nearby, but had given up looking for them. They consoled themselves by shredding the remaining book and dismantled all the book shelves left behind.

Once the kiwis had lost interest in the cave and returned to their usual routines, Kohana took Oreana back into the cave. They were able to rescue some of the slates and chalky rocks they used for writing. The punga and branches used for shelves and seating were also collected for use in their new school too.

There was delight the night the new school was opened for all the animals who had missed their previous classes. Oreana asked for volunteers to help run the classes as she would have to nest soon. A male Ruru, Orok from their community took over the classes.

KIRWINA ESCAPES

Kirwina sniffed as she exited her burrow. Moisture was in the air. She knew that rain was coming soon. Kirwina couldn't see them, but she knew she was being watched. Ever since Kamoku had left, Kirwina had found herself being followed. There was another year before she was old enough to breed. Kirwina hoped that she wouldn't be forced into mating before she was ready.

As Kirwina ventured into the feeding area, she came across Kera, a female her own age, who was looking very miserable.

"What is wrong?" Kirwina asked as they fed together.

Kera looked around furtively before answering.

"One of the males tried to force himself on me. I managed to fight him off, but I don't know how long I can keep him at bay."

Kirwina nodded her understanding. "I've had someone following me too. I don't know how long I will be left in peace either. Perhaps we should keep together. It will be harder for them to force us to submit when there are two of us to fight them off."

Kirwina checked Kera's burrow. It was larger than her own, but it was in the middle of the community. It would be almost impossible to escape from there without someone knowing. Kirwina encouraged Kera to share her burrow, which was on the slope of the hill, near the edge of the community. It was drier than most of the other burrows and sheltered from the weather.

"We can make it bigger so it is more comfortable for us both."

While they were discussing the merits of her burrow, a shadow came over the entrance.

"What's going on?" The voice was from one of the males. Kera shrank behind Kirwina as he spoke. Kirwina realised this was the male that tried to mate with Kera.

Kirwina stepped boldly forward, giving him a withering stare.

"We aren't ready for mating yet, so to protect ourselves, we are going to share. Go find a female that is ready."

The male gave Kirwina a sullen look, before sloping off.

"Thank you!" Kera expressed her relief. "I wish I.." Kirwina stopped her. She was sure that someone was listening outside. She shot outside and raked her claw through the ferns in front of her. When her claw made contact with something solid, there was a yelp and a flurry of movement through the ferns, as the listener fled. Kirwina waited a few minutes. All remained quiet. If anyone else was around, they were keeping out of sight.

"You want to leave?" Kirwina spoke this in a whisper in case anyone else was hanging around.

Kera nodded.

"We will have to wait till everyone is asleep. In the meantime, we need to get out and feed well. We will stay closer to our burrow in case anyone tries to make a move on us."

During the next few hours the rain set in. At first

Kirwina and Kera ignored it, but when a thunder storm arrived, they went for shelter along with everyone else. Dawn was breaking when the weather finally passed towards the Alps.   Many kiwis nipped out for a quick feed before the sun came up, but Kirwina and Kera had chosen to settle early; remained in their burrow, sleeping.

During the day some showers came through. It was during a shower that Kirwina and Kera made their move. Keeping away from all the other burrows in their area, they climbed up to the top of the ridge to hide under some King ferns. There was no sign of anyone following them, so continued on their way, feeding as they went.

As dusk settled on the Paparoa range, both Kirwina and Kera were feeling tired, but carried on at a slower pace.   The further they travelled, the more confident Kirwina and Kera felt that they were now safe.

After a few hours they made a temporary burrow to rest, rising in the early morning to travel some more. Only when the daylight was bright did they sleep for the day.

Back at the community there was anger that two females had successfully vanished from sight. The two males who had been following Kirwina and Kera were sent with several others to Three Sisters Mountain. They had orders to bring them back, or kill them if they refused to return.

The first that Kuaka and Kamoku knew of the raiding party heading their way, was when Odion the Ruru leader at Three Sisters' flew in to the school.

"We have some visitors coming from the south." Odion announced.

The whole community gathered together as the kiwis made their way up the mountainside. The grim faces told Kuaka that this wasn't a social visit.

"Stop!" Kuaka shouted at them as they came nearer. "Why are you here?"

"We are here for Kirwina and Kera. Give them to us or you will suffer with them!"

"They aren't here! Are you sure they came this way?"

"We are coming to check you aren't hiding them from us!"

"I will escort one of you for a check. The rest of you stay where you are!"

Kuaka ordered Kamoku and half the males to guard the remaining males in the party. The remaining males came with Kuaka and the leading male to inspect the community burrows and the school. After their inspection, the leading male was returned to his party, who were sitting in sullen silence after Kamoku had made them sit still. He had not trusted them to move around on the pretext of feeding while they waited.

"Do you think they have gone north?" the leading male was now worried. The Buller community had a fierce reputation that even they wouldn't challenge.

"I doubt it, but you can check if you're game. If they are up there, you won't be getting them back."

After the kiwis moved off the mountain, Kuaka asked Odion to check which way they went. If they headed towards the Ohikanui river, Kerwin's group would have to be warned. To Kuaka's relief, the kiwis returned to their community.

Kirwina and Kera continued on their journey to the south, grateful that no-one was following them. Kamoku had told Kirwina about the family home that he wanted to visit someday. His father Kanoa had visited it many years ago. Kanoa had met Kamoku's mother Koana there.

At the Three Sisters Mountain, Kamoku was relieved that Kirwina had escaped from the community, but he was also worried. If Kirwina and Kera weren't coming this way, where were they going? Kamoku saw a Wood Pigeon/Kereru nearby that he recognised as Pippi. He also knew that the Kereru had a network throughout the Island. There was little that they didn't know about.

"Pippi, can you find out where Kirwina and Kera are heading?"

"You want to join them?"

"I do."

The next evening, Kirwina and Kera were emerging from their temporary burrow, when a Kereru came to sit on a nearby branch.

"Are you Kirwina and Kera?" it asked.

"Who wants to know?" Kirwina asked anxiously.

"Kamoku. He wants to join you."

"Tell him we are going to his old family home."

Kerwin looked out of his burrow. The water level in the Ohikanui river was still high after the flooding the previous night.

The community had settled in well in the valley, but Kerwin had seen the high tide mark and was glad that all the burrows were made above it. There had been much scrambling to reach safety when the flood waters roared through while they were feeding. After checking that everyone was safe, they continued their feeding high on the slopes.

Now Kerwin was feeling restless, and wondered whether the community was also having second thoughts on staying in this valley. He didn't have long to find out. As Kerwin led his family out of their burrow, including two week old Karri, members of the community were waiting for him.

"You want to move on?" Kerwin asked them.

There were nods of relief that he understood how they felt. "I know of a lake where there is a school already set up for us to go to, though humans and their animals live next to the water. It is a long walk from here. Are you interested? The other alternative is up in the mountains where there is snow in winter.

"Do other kiwis live at the lake?

"Not now. The school was set up by Keoni, the first leader of the Kiwi Kingdom and his friend a Ruru, who became the first guardian of the kingdom. Other animals including spirit harriers attend it now.

"Spirit Harriers? What are they doing in the living world?"

"I would like to know too!" Kerwin grinned at his community. "By the sound of it they are causing some trouble for the local animals who could do with our help."

There were grins from the males in his community who were happy to help keep the harriers in line.

"You are ready to go now?"

The smiles on their faces told Kerwin they were. They took their time as they set out on their journey. There were a number of new members in the community, some of them still learning to feed. The local Ruru saw them, and called ahead to Odion at Three Sisters Mountain.

Kamoku was with Kuaka when Odion brought the news that Kerwin and the community were heading their way.

"Find out where they are heading." Kuaka told Odion. He turned to Kamoku. "Don't leave yet, you may be leading Kerwin's community to their new home. It would be best to head east to the Grey valley."

A few nights later, Kamoku was led by Odion to meet Kerwin and his community.

Kamoku greeted Kerwin with a smile.

"You are going to my old family home."

"You have been there before?"

"No, but my father has visited it. My great Uncle Keoni started the Kingdom there. Kuaka has told me to lead you down the inland side of these mountains. It will be safer. I am meeting my future mate who is heading for the Kaniere community."

"You were already heading there?"

"I was. I heard she had escaped from the community where I grew up, in these mountains. The kereru were able to find her and tell me where she was going."

"Why did you leave your community?"

"When dad died, mum wanted to leave. I was still young then, so when Kotare and his friends came to visit our community on their way home to Three Sisters community, they invited us to go with them. Mum is settled at Three Sisters Community now. I know I can't go back now, as some members from my old community came and tried to force me to return. I know they wanted to eliminate me."

"I've been in your situation recently." Kerwin spoke in sympathy. Can you lead us on a safe path?"

"I can. I have checked the atlas at our school. It means climbing to the top of this valley, then down the other side, which will lead us to the inland side of this range. My old community doesn't go there."

"How long do you think it will take us to reach Kaniere?" One of the kiwis wanted to know.

Kamoku looked at the new crescent moon.

"Probably the next moon will be full before we reach it."

Once the community had traversed the ridge at the top of the Ohikanui, they found their journey much more sheltered on this side. Both Kerwin and Kamoku noticed that both Kereru and Ruru would come and go,

41

as they continued on their way.

"Someone is keeping an eye on us." Kerwin mentioned to Kamoku one morning as they prepared to sleep for the day. He agreed.

"Kuaka has probably sent the Kereru to give an update on our progress, and Koa has probably sent the Ruru as well."

"You think so?" Kerwin brightened at the mention of Koa's name.

"Don't be surprised if there is a welcoming party when we arrive. Dad used to talk about the big parties they've had there for their celebrations and commemorations. Your community coming to live at the home of the Kingdom, is a big event to celebrate."

"Do you think Koa will be there?"

"I would guarantee it!

Further down the coast, Kirwina and Kera had reached the Cobden lagoon. They found a sheltered spot for their burrow, away from the path where humans and their dogs came for their walks. They were lulled to sleep, to the sound of the sea pounding on the coast. Rain clouds gathered on the horizon.

Their journey that night was is drenching rain. A benefit of the wet conditions, was that all the dogs in the settlement were being kept indoors. The streets were also quiet as they made their way to the bridge over Greymouth River, which was in flood. Kirwina and Kera crossed it swiftly, grateful they didn't need to swim this river. They skirted the town in the bushland, to make their way south to Paroa. The river there also was in flood, so found a spot high on the hill to shelter for the day.

As Kamoku and Kerwin's community made their way down the Grey valley, they too, had to keep to the slopes away from the river which was now in flood. There was a number of creeks and streams that needed to be crossed. The young ones receiving lessons on how to swim in moving water.

The night they came across the bridge to cross the Grey River, Kamoku turned to Kerwin with a smile.

"It shouldn't take us long to reach Lake Kaniere now. We have a few streams and a couple of rivers to cross; they have bridges."

Kerwin looked at the new crescent moon.

Kamoku nodded as he too looked at the moon.

"We should be there when it is full."

Kirwina and Kera crossed the Arahura river bridge to make their way up stream. They deliberately kept away from the road that humans had made in the valley. It was only when they came across another gravel road leading to the lake and Mount Tuhua, that they followed it.

By now all the animals at the lake had been put on alert for any Kiwis heading their way. Wesley Weka was having a forage in the forest in Hans Bay when he heard the footsteps of two animals he didn't know. Instinct made him slip behind the nearest tree, as they passed by. To his surprise, here was two female Kiwis who were alone.

"Hello." Wesley called out to them. "Where are you heading?"

Kirwina and Kea turned around to see the

twinkling eyes of a Weka smiling at them. Kirwina smiled back.

"Is Kamoku here yet? He was going to show me his family home."

"Not yet, but we are expecting him, and Kerwin's community. Would you like to see the burrow that his great grandfather made for the family?"

Kirwina's eyes shone. She hadn't expected it to be here still. Keeping close to Wesley as he skirted around the properties than now inhabited the forest, he led them to a Pepper bush, pulling aside the lower branches to reveal an entrance.

"Here is one entrance." He then led them to a nearby stream where many ferns now grew. "Here is another one." Wesley pulled aside the ferns to show the opening in the bank.

As Wesley was showing Kirwina and Kera the burrow, Protea, a local Kereru happened to pass by. The sight of the two Kiwis sent her flying to the school cave, to spread the news of the new arrivals.

"Come in." Wesley invited them to follow him. He had been in this burrow and others he had found when he came to live in this area. Wesley had heard that Keoni kiwi's spirit was still around, but he hadn't revealed himself to him.

Swiftly Kirwina and Kera followed Wesley into the dark tunnels. It took a while to adjust to the darkness in here, listening intently to the sound of Wesley's footsteps in front of them. Kirwina liked the feel of the soft moss under her feet. As she slowly was able to discern Wesley's shape, he stopped, to look at something in a side tunnel. Kirwina and Kera joined him, astonished to see the bright green outline of a large claw on the back wall.

"Who made it?" Kirwina wanted to know.

"Keoni did." Wesley spoke with pride.

"That's Kamoku's great uncle!" Kirwina exclaimed. Isn't he the one that began the Kiwi Kingdom?"

"He did!" Wesley confirmed. "This is his symbol for the Kingdom."

"Thank you for showing us. Kamoku will love to see it too, when he gets here."

They could hear some animals calling for Wesley outside, so he swiftly led them out the other entrance, under the Pepper bush.

"Wesley! What are you doing in Keoni's tunnels?" came the reproving tone from a Ruru sitting on a nearby branch, as he led Kirwina and Kera out of the burrow. Wesley gave a cheeky grin as he introduced the two kiwis to the crowd surrounding the bush.

"Kirwina and Kera, meet our community." He then explained to the crowd. "Kirwina and Kera are here to meet Kamoku when he gets here. They are from Kamoku's community.

"Are you going to stay?" two Weasels came running up to them with grins on their faces.

"We are!" Kirwina smiled back at them.

"Good! Would you like to see the school or the lake first?"

"You can show them the lake and school later, Wahi. We will take them to a suitable burrow first, and

45

let them settle in."

Kirwina looked at the branch above. Sitting on it was a large family of Ruru. In other branches were fantails, Tuis, Waxeyes, Robins and Bellbirds. Running towards them was a family of stoats, followed by Hedgehogs and some possums. She saw movement in the branch of the next tree. A large Harrier in white feathers had settled there, and was staring at them intently.

During the chaos of all the introductions, she completely forgot about the harrier. Kirwina and Kera were led up the mountainside, where Wesley showed them some old burrows that had been used in Keoni's reign. After choosing one, they went out to feed. Before Wesley left, he promised to show them where the school was after their rest time. As they fed, Kera and Kirwina were given glimpses of a large body of water through the trees. In the early morning light is seemed mysterious as the peak they could see on the opposite shore.

When Kamoku and Kerwin came to the Arahura River, they were glad they had a bridge to cross the swift flowing river. The final leg of the journey had been through thick forest, with many streams to cross. Kamoku spotted some deer in a nearby field, wondering whether they were part of the kingdom. His father Kanoa had told him of the deer that had given him a ride from their home at Paparoa range, down to this lake. Kamoku also realised that he wouldn't be returning to the Paparoa Range ever again. That this lake was to be his forever home now. Kerwin saw Kamoku's reflective mood, asking him what was up.

46

"I was just thinking that there is no going back. We are nearly at our forever home" Kamoku smiled at Kerwin.

Kerwin nodded his agreement. He also had sadness in his eyes, acknowledging he was missing his old home.

"Nothing and no-one is going to make us leave this one!" Kerwin said with determination.

"Agreed!" Kamoku was equally determined.

They guessed that the gravel road would lead them to the lake, following it over the ridge as they travelled through the forest.

Frangipani Fantail was sleeping on her nest, when she heard and saw a large number of Kiwis approaching. She immediately dropped down to the ground in front of them.

"Hello! Are you Kamoku and Kerwin's community?"

Kamoku stopped and smiled at the Fantail, who was chatting to them excitedly.

"We are." Kamoku confirmed. "Is Kirwina here?"

"She certainly is!" Frangipani put out a loud call,

"They are here!" which was answered in the distance. "Follow me! The community will be here shortly." Within minutes, the kiwis found themselves surrounded by Ruru, Kereru and Tuis. They could hear animals approaching on the ground. Leading them was Kirwina and Kera.

"Welcome home!" Kirwina called as she rushed into Kamoku's embrace.

MEETING HAGAR

Kerwin and his community were amazed at the welcome they received from all the animals that came to meet them. Kirwina and Kera led them all to the school where another surprise was waiting. Koa and his family were also here!

As Kerwin went over to greet Koa, he noticed that Koa had aged a great deal. Old battle scars were also obvious on his face. One thing that hadn't changed was the grin Koa gave him.

"Nice of you all to drop in." Koa said in an understatement. "I take it you are staying?"

"That's the plan." Kerwin's grin matched Koa's. Kerwin motioned Kamoku to join them and introduced him.

"You aren't any relation to Keoni and Kupe's family by any chance?"

"Yes. Keoni's father Kamoku came to our Paparoa community when he left here. He is my great, great Grandfather."

How is it up there?" Koa wanted to know.

Mum took me to Three Sisters community after dad died. I had a visit from some of the Kiwis at Paparoa recently, demanding I go back with them. I refused, as I suspected they wanted to eliminate me. Luckily Kuaka was there to back me up. When I heard that Kirwina had escaped from Paparoa and was heading here, I chose to join her." He looked at Kerwin. "Kerwin's community was heading this way too, so I gave them an escort."

"Welcome home Kamoku. You will be wanting to see Kamoku's old burrow. Kirwina will be able to show it to you." Koa turned to Kerwin. "Welcome to your new home too. Let me know if you have any problems."

"I will do, though we are looking forward to being settled in one place at last. We were driven out of the Tasman, though I hear there aren't enough of them left for a viable community now. We weren't welcome at the Buller, which I understand, given the previous leader Kaine was responsible for the death of your father Kehi. We found the Ohikanui valley nice and quiet, but it tends to flood. We decided it would be good to come here, as this community doesn't have any Kiwis to protect them, and it has a school already set up here too."

Koa grinned when Kerwin mentioned protection of the Kaniere comunity, his eyes moving to the corner of the cave. Kerwin and Kamoku followed his gaze, to a white harrier who was sitting watching the crowd of new arrivals mingle with the local animals. The Harrier seemed to know that someone was looking at him, He turned his gaze on Koa, Kerwin and Kamoku.

"I will introduce you." Koa said as he led them over to the harrier.

"Hagar," meet Kerwin the leader of the Kiwi Community, and Kamoku. Kamoku's family led the community here in the past. He has come home."

Hagar looked at Kerwin and Kamoku with a penetrating stare, which they met with an equal penetrating look, to let him know they were not afraid.

"How long are you here?"

"We all are here to stay. This is our home now."

Both Kerwin and Kamoku saw a flash of anger in the harrier's eyes, which passed as quickly as it came.

"Welcome." Hagar said as two Ruru came to land next to Kerwin and Kamoku.

"We haven't introduced ourselves properly." One spoke. "I'm Oriel the guardian of the Kingdom and this is Oregon. He is the leader of the spirit world."

Oregon grinned at the startled looks from both Kerwin and Kamoku, that a living Ruru was the leader of the spirit world.

"I'm fully connected to the spirit world. I can see and communicate with the animals there." Oregon explained.

"Your community will be attending the school?" Oriel asked.

"Yes, We certainly will!" Kerwin replied with enthusiasm. "We have missed it on our travels here. I'm just glad that one is already set up for us here. I'm sad though that the one I set up will be lost."

"I have some good news for you." Oriel said. "The school you set up is safe and has been moved to a new location."

"It has?" Kerwin's eyes lit up. His joy at this news was evident.

"Would you like to help at this school?" Oriel asked. Odele was going to nest soon. He would be able to help her more if he had some free time.

"I would love to."

"Come along to the class tonight."

As Oriel Kerwin and Kamoku prepared to leave the cave, Kamoku noticed that Hagar stayed behind.

"Hagar aren't you coming?" Kamoku called to him.   Hagar gave him a withering look.

"I stay here!"

"Not anymore you don't!" Kamoku was adamant.

"What gives you the right to dictate whether I stay or not?"

Kamoku tapped the floor of the cave, before sweeping his claw in a big circle.

"This cave, this lake and the hills and mountains around it are MY territory! My family ruled this territory long before you came. I am here to make sure it STAYS in my family! Before you joined the Kingdom, you had a territory. It is time you returned to it. We will expect you at class tomorrow." Kamoku pointed his claw at the Harrier before moving it towards the cave entrance. Reluctantly the Harrier left the cave to leave the area. There was silence for a few seconds after the Harrier departed.

"Thank you, Kamoku." Oriel expressed his gratitude. "Hagar had taken over this space. He seemed to think it gave him power."

"I thought he had." Kamoku was thoughtful. "But the power he seeks isn't something he will ever get. The Kingdom doesn't work that way."

"No it doesn't." Oriel agreed. "It's time we joined our females."

As Oriel led Kamoku and Kerwin out of the cave, above them, Kanoa looked at Keoni, Kupe and Kaori with a grin.

"I wouldn't have missed that for anything. Old Kamoku would be proud of him."

"We all are!" Keoni spoke. "We will have to be vigilant and make sure Kamoku is protected. Hagar won't be happy that the power he felt by being in the cave has been taken from him."

SETTLING IN

Kamoku found Kirwina and Kera waiting for him as he left the school cave. They led him up the mountainside to where they were sharing a burrow. A smaller burrow had been dug next door. Other Kiwis were furiously digging their burrows before daylight came.

"You've made this for me? I really appreciate it!"

Kirwina couldn't help showing her surprise.

"You don't want to start our relationship?"

Kamoku came over to give Kirwina a cuddle.

"I know you have another year before you are fully ready to carry our family. I am happy to wait till you are ready for it." He gave her a tender smile. Tears of relief and joy came to Kirwina's eyes. "It's a good idea for you both to keep sharing till you are ready." Kamoku turned to check out the burrow they had made for him. Fresh ferns had been laid inside. One of the other unattached males sidled up to Kamoku's burrow.

"You aren't going with Kirwina?"

Kamoku smiled at him. "I will when she is ready. She and Kera are too young to mate yet."

Kamoku saw a look of surprise come over his face.

"They left my old community because the males there were trying to force them into mating before they were ready."

"I'm Koron. Can I share with you? I like to have company in my burrow."

"I don't like being alone either." Kamoku grinned at him and moved aside to make room for him. Then another two Kiwis, Kiro and Kena came along, peering into their burrow.

"That's where you are Koron. Is there any room for us?"

"We will have to make this bigger if you want to share."

Much digging later, the burrow was big enough for the four of them to settle. The early morning sunlight was touching Conical Hill.

When Kamoku woke that evening, dusk was settling on the lake. Kirwina was waiting for him.

"You want to see the family burrow?" she asked quietly, after he crept out to join her. He nodded. Leading him down the steep slopes, they passed Kerwin and his family who also were out feeding.

"Are you going down to the lake?" Kerwin asked hopefully. He was nervous about exploring down by the water, knowing that humans and their animals were also there. Kamoku stopped, looking at Kirwina. Their visit to his family burrow wasn't going to be private after all.

"We are heading that way." Kirwina smiled.

Behind them, they could hear footsteps coming in a hurry. It was Koron with Kiro and Kena.

"Where are you going?" Koron wanted to know.

"For a look at the water."

"Aren't there humans and their animals down there?" Kiro asked nervously.

"Yes, but there are enough of us here to defend ourselves if any human's animals try to attack us."

"What about the humans?"

"We are protected. Humans aren't allowed to

harm us. We are going anyway. You can stay up here if you want."

With that Kirwina and Kamoku set off down the slopes. Kerwin and his family followed them. Looking at each other, Koron, Kiro and Kena followed them nervously, before the others disappeared out of sight. Down on the flat, Kirwina stopped by a road. She listened carefully before leading them across to a gap in the trees. In front of them lay a large body water, now dark in the fading light. It was surrounded by thick forest. A large hill dominated the landscape on the other side of the lake.

A splash in the water by the water's edge announced the arrival of an eel. Koron, Kiro and Kena shrank back in fear, but Kirwina ran forward to it.

"Hello Eli. I have brought some of our new arrivals down to see the lake."

"Hello Kirwina. Are you going to introduce them?"

As Kirwina introduced the Kiwi's, more eels came to join Eli. One of them, Ernie asked Kamoku if he knew of Keoni.

"Of course! Keoni is my great uncle. His father was my great, great grandfather."

"Welcome home Kamoku!"

As Kirwina led them back through the forest towards Tuhua, they heard a hiss behind them. Kamoku immediately turned to face the cat that was confronting them, with its claw up. Kamoku also put his claw up. Kirwina and Kerwin immediately joined him, with their claws up.

"Who are you?" Kamoku asked. "Why are you

being hostile? We live here now, so you need to get on with us."

The cat wasn't used to other animals talking to them, just hissed and growled some more.

Kamoku stepped forward and raked the cat across the face. With a scream, the cat turned and ran away, with Kamoku and Kirwina following close behind them. It wasn't till the cat ran onto the veranda of a home and disappeared inside through a cat flap that they were satisfied it wouldn't bother them again tonight. Kirwina led Kamoku back to the others, who had waited where Kamoku and Kirwina had left them.

"Are there many more of those around?" Koron wanted to know.

"Not many." Kirwina reassured him. "Most of them stay close to home and are easy to deal with. It is the dogs we have to be careful of. Most humans control them, but there are some who let them run wild."

When Kirwina led them into the school cave, all the other kiwis were already there, waiting for them, along with the local animals they would come to know as friends.

"Sorry we are late." Kirwina began. "We have just been down to see Ernie and the eels. One of the local cats was sent home on the way back."

ODELIA'S RETURN

Oreana the Ruru was about to leave the nesting hollow, when Odelia's voice came loud in her head.

"STOP! Something is here!"

Oreana barely had time to retreat back into the hollow next to Oren, when a large white claw reached into the hollow, just missing Oren.

"A Spirit Harrier is here! Get behind me!" Oreana told Oren. He quickly obeyed. Odelia then screamed out.

HAINA!

Her scream had an immediate effect in the spirit world. Everyone now knew that Odelia was back! – and she needed help! Spirit animals rushed to the location of the scream. At Nudoor, Hirone the Haast Eagle looked for Haina, but Haina had already disappeared from view. Hirone saw Haera and Hiena, the guardian eagles for Oregon and his mate Ophena. He nodded to them. They too, disappeared from view.

Oregon was in his position, on top of Mount Tuhua, counselling a spirit world stoat when he heard his mother's scream. Both Oregon and the stoat looked towards the call.

How can it be, that Odelia is back? The stoat asked Oregon.

I want to know too! Oregon replied.

He felt something land behind him.

Who is it? Oregon asked, as he turned; ready to

strike if he was attacked.

Its Haera. I'm here to protect you."

Thank you!

The first Ophena knew of the situation, was feeling something heavy land on the branch she was sitting on. She looked around to find no-one was visible. Thinking it might be a Harrier, she swiftly shuffled away, ready to flee.

"Who is it? What do you want?"

It is Hiena. I am here to protect you. Odelia has returned, but she is in danger. You could be in danger too. Hiena's words boomed in Ophena's head.

Thank you!

Both Oregon and Ophena now had to readjust, how they moved through the forest, so their Eagles could either be with, or see them at all times.

At the nesting hollow, Oreana's eyes had changed. Minjarra the Marsupial lion now looked out on her world. She also had the lion's strength to match. Oreana grabbed the Harrier's claw and slammed it into the side of the hollow; holding it there, till a much stronger force yanked it from her grasp.

When Kohana and Titan arrived, Oreana could hear Titan's growl outside, but both Kohana and Titan were swept aside, as a much bigger claw came to snatch the luckless Harrier. The Harrier screamed as it's spirit was crushed and its feathers scattered, to disappear in the breeze.

In the Kaniere school cave, Hagar also heard Odelia's cry for Haina and looked at Oriel with incredulous eyes. He was still angry at being removed from the cave, but hadn't decided yet, what to do about it.

"What is it?" Oriel asked, seeing the astonished look on Hagar's face.

"I've just heard Odelia call for Haina!"

"Are you sure?"

"I'm sure."

When the sound of the Harrier's scream came to Hagar, he left the cave. As he gained height, Hagar saw Oregon on the mountain top and went to join him. The stoat swiftly left as the harrier came in to land.

Did you hear her?

Yes. Did you hear your harrier?

I did.

In Hagar was an anger that he could not conceal. He attempted to lash out with his claw, to take Oregon's life. To his surprise, Oregon's claw gripped his with a strength of an animal much bigger than he was. In Oregon's eyes was the strange light he had seen before.

Hagar then tried to strike Oregon with his beak. He felt fear for the first time as a much bigger claw came to envelop his upper body, including his head.

I have him.

As Haera lifted Hagar, Hagar tried to strike Oregon with his other foot. Oregon found he had to hold onto both of Hagar's legs to stop him from injuring both him and his eagle. Oregon could also sense that another Harrier was nearby, which made him vulnerable to attack.

On the other side of the Tasman, Minjarra the marsupial lion could also see and sense what Oregon was seeing and feeling. He was already on his way to help him, when Oregon called to Hirone.

Hirone! We need help! Oregon kept looking round behind him in case he was attacked from behind.

Hirone sent Hira down to Mount Tuhua.

As Hira appeared, Minjarra also arrived; just in time to grab the harrier, that was launching itself at Oregon.   Hearing the commotion behind him, as Minjarra subdued the harrier, Oregon was relieved, when Hira's claw closed round the Harrier's legs in an iron grip.

You can let go now.

As soon as Oregon released his grip and moved away, Haera and Hira crushed Hagar, scattering his feathers. They looked around at Minjarra, who had a satisfied look on his face as he consumed the remains of the other harrier.

Thank you Minjarra Oregon spoke as the lion disappeared from view, a single feather held in his mouth. Another visit to the great plain (the Nullarbor) was called for!

Back at Oreana and Oren's nesting hollow, Oreana and Oren emerged to find the area surrounded by spirit animals, including Kohana and Titan.

"All the spirit animals are here." Oreana told Oren.

Thank you all for coming. We are safe now.

Where is she? Manu the Moa spoke. *We all heard her call out for Haina!*

Oreana smiled and waited for her mother to speak.

I am here! I am now part of Oreana.

Are you going to be spirit leader again? Moana the Moa wanted to know.

Not unless I need to. I am enjoying being an ordinary ruru again. Oregon is serving you well, isn't he?

He is.

As Moana spoke, Oregon could be heard calling to Hirone for help. All eyes turned to the south west anxiously, before the sound of Harrier screams were heard, reassuring them that Oregon was now safe.

We have been given protection again, so you don't have to worry about our safety. Oreana reassured the crowd. She turned to Oren as the crowd dispersed.

"I'm ready for a feed now."

It wasn't long before Hirone received a visit.

You have seen her?

Yes. She is part of Oreana now. Oregon is to remain our leader.

In the Westland forests, a spirit harrier realised that they were now all alone in this kingdom. Turning towards the Alps, and keeping well clear of Nudoor, they headed for Canterbury. As the harrier allowed the wind to carry him over the passes to the Canterbury plain, he was joined by another harrier.

Welcome! We didn't think there were any left over there.

There aren't! I'm the last one.

THE BURROW

The Kiwis from the Tasman appreciated being in a class again and reading books they hadn't seen before. Kamoku and Kirwina sat together, while Kera sat with some of the unattached females from the Tasman. Kerwin helped Oriel with the class, which was much bigger than usual. Once the class was over, everyone filed out for the important activity of the night – to feed. Kerwin had noticed that Oregon had been missing from the classes and mentioned the fact to Oriel.

"I know." Oriel replied sadly. "He wants to come, but his duties as leader of the Spirit world keep him busy during our class time. He then has to help his mate Ophena raise their family, which doesn't give him any time to come here."

"Where does Oregon conduct his spirit world duties?" Kerwin wanted to know.

"Up on top of this mountain." He could see that Kerwin was trying to find a way to bring the classes to Oregon. "What are you thinking?"

"We take turns at taking the classes. On the night you take them, I will go up the mountain early to give Oregon a lesson. Can you ask him what he thinks?"

"I will." Oriel smiled. He already knew what Oregon would say.

When Kamoku and Kirwina left the school cave, they quietly made their way down the mountain side, feeding as they went. The possum family also was heading that way too, but they were heading for Terry and Amy's garden, to see what flowers fruit or vegetables, were available for them to eat. Kamoku and Kirwina noticed the possum family head towards the gardens where humans lived. Another time they would go with them to see what could be found there.

Kirwina led Kamoku through the forest, to the Pepper bush. They could see the lights of the nearby house were on. Ducking underneath, she led Kamoku into the tunnels. When they came to the wall where Keoni had blocked off the tunnel, Kamoku felt confused.

"What happened here?" Kamoku spoke without thinking. "There should be a tunnel here."

Before Kirwina could answer, a voice spoke behind them.

"There was, but it was blocked off."

They both looked round to see a spirit kiwi was with them. Kamoku could only guess which member of the family was here.

"Welcome home, Kamoku." The kiwi spoke. "I'm Keoni. I blocked the tunnel off as my mother is buried in the tunnel there."

Keoni went on to explain how he had to protect both his mother and the burrow for the family.

"Where did you sleep?" Kamoku wanted to know.

"Allow me." Keoni passed them to lead the way. As they came closer to the stream, Keoni stopped at a smaller tunnel. Kamoku looked in silence at the claw marked in the wall, filled with moss.

"Isn't that symbol on a book in the library?"

"It is." Keoni grinned at Kamoku. "My best friend Orion made that book, to leave for the next leader of the

63

Kingdom, which was Kupe. His daughter Kohana was the next leader before Koa."

"Did someone mention my name?"

They looked around to see another spirit kiwi behind them.

"Kamoku, meet Kupe. He used to live in the family burrow too."

"Yes, I slept in this tunnel too. Are you going to live here, Kamoku?"

"I don't think so." Kamoku said sadly. "The humans and their animals are too close. We have made our burrows up on the mountain where we feel safer."

"We understand." Kupe replied. "Both Keoni's and my community left this lake, after humans and their animals came to live here. You should be safe up on the mountain."

"We have no intention of moving anywhere!" Kamoku's voice was firm. Outside, they could hear Koron Kiro and Kena calling for them.

"It's time for us to go. That's my mates calling for us."

"We will see you again." Kupe farewelled them before both Kupe and Keoni disappeared from view.

"This way." Kirwina spoke as she led Kamoku out to the stream.

"We are here!" Kirwina called to Koron.

"What have you been doing?" Koron wanted to know. "You snuck away really quick!"

"We've just been looking at an old family burrow. Do you want to have a look at the lake?"

Kamoku didn't mention it, but he could see

humans looking at them from the fence at their property. They must have heard them calling. As Kamoku led Kirwina and his friends to the lake shore, the couple looked at each other in amazement.

"You were right!" he spoke. "We will have to tell everyone to keep their dogs on leads. It explains why the cat came tearing in and won't go outside again!"

By the water's edge, the lake was dark. The forest in the bay was a black silhouette, against the moonless sky, which was filled with stars. Kirwina and Kamoku wadded in for a paddle, to find themselves surrounded by eels.

"Hello Kirwina and Kamoku!" It was Ernie. "Are you joining us for a swim?"

"Maybe a short one in the bay. We only came for a paddle." Kamoku looked around at his mates with a grin, before plunging in. Kirwina followed him in, to find Eli next to her, asking how she was enjoying her life here. Koron, Kiro and Kena slowly followed them, finding themselves surrounded by eels, asking where they had come from and if they were staying. By the time they all emerged from the water, some new friendships had been made, with promises to return soon for another swim with them.

In the forest, Oriel was sitting next to Oregon, who was looking at him with incredulous eyes.

"Kerwin is going to do that for me?"

"He is. You will have to show me where you have your sessions, so we can take some slates and books up for your lessons. Is there any protected spots nearby to store things?"

After some thought, Oregon remembered. "There is a hollow at the base of a nearby tree where we can store things."

In the forest, Kerwin was feeding with Karamu. Their children were off feeding with the friends they had made in the school classes.

"I will be up early every second evening." Kerwin informed her. "I will be up the top of the mountain helping Oregon with his lessons."

"You will have to show me." Karamu smiled at him. "It must be a nice view up there."

"Come up with us." Kerwin invited her. "The children are independent now."

"Will you be up there tonight?" Karamu asked, "Maybe we could go up and sleep there this morning? We can come back down after your lesson."

Kerwin and Karamu started making their way up the mountain slopes, finding the path that humans had made much easier to climb. On reaching the top, they looked along the ridge, wondering where Oregon held his meetings, when the unmistakeable shape of Oriel came flying up from the forest. He had a slate in his beak. He headed for a tree further along the ridge. By the time Kerwin and Karamu reached the tree, Oriel had departed again. They saw a rock with views nearby and guessed this was where Oregon met the spirit animals.

Choosing the base of a large tree nearby, they started to dig a burrow.

"What are you doing?" Oriel was behind them.

"We are just making ourselves comfortable." Kerwin grinned at Oriel. "I will be ready when Oregon comes up this evening."

When Oregon arrived that evening, he was soaking wet from the driving rain. He was very grateful for the shelter of the burrow which was protected from the weather. As the lesson progressed, his memory of the lessons Odelia had given him and Oleander in the park in Sydney, came back to him.

At the end of the lesson, Kerwin commented.

"What you need now is some books, though it will be difficult to get them up here. I will see Oriel. He will know what to do."

After Kerwin and Karamu ducked out, to make the now treacherous climb back down the wet and slippery slopes to their community, Oregon started to receive his spirit animals, who also appreciated this new meeting place, out of the weather. They too, were interested to hear about the lessons Oregon was having.

At their community, Kerwin and Karamu were surrounded by anxious neighbours, wanting to know where they had been. They calmed down after Kerwin explained he had been on top of the mountain to sleep, and give Oregon a lesson; and that he would be straight down again afterwards. Kerwin also told them, that he would be taking the lessons on the nights, when Oriel was spending time helping his mate.

At the school cave, Oriel was just about to leave, when Kerwin came bolting down the stairs.

"How did it go?" Oriel asked, though the smile on Kerwin's face told him that the session had been successful.

"He remembered most of the things Odelia taught him in his other life." Kerwin was being careful what he said, as he didn't know who or what was listening. "He needs some books. Is there any way of getting some up to him?"

"I will ask Amy."

MEETING KERWIN

Hoani was playing in the back garden at the bach with Alice and Naku her younger brother, while Lucy was making their dinner. It wouldn't be long before dusk turned to nightfall.

Both Hoani and Lucy had been extra busy recently with their careers. They felt the need to get away from everything and managed to get a week off together. Clearing their diaries, they loaded up their car and made the trip out to the bach at Hans Bay. Terry and Amy would be bringing their children Jimmy and Emily out tomorrow, for the weekend.

Hoani spotted the Ruru sitting on the branch over the shed. It seemed to be alone. He didn't see the kiwi hiding in the shed, where Oriel had led him.

In the shed Kerwin was looking around with interest. It seemed to be another school room! The floor was covered with a strange smelling mat, which was softer than most things on the forest floor. Some cardboard boxes held books. He recognised the slates and chalk that was used in their school. Some other boxes were turned up, Kerwin presumed to sit on. This was a very comfortable set up! He would have to ask Oriel who was using this space.

Kerwin heard a human voice from the house call out, before the Human and the children went indoors. Kerwin felt more comfortable now that darkness was descending over the forest. Then Kerwin heard Oriel give him a soft call to come with him.

As Kerwin came round the side of the shed to join Oriel, he was anxious to find the humans had left a light on outside on the veranda.

"Are you sure it's safe here?" Kerwin asked anxiously, squinting in the light.

"Yes. I've been here many times." Oriel reassured him. "Amy's daughter Lucy is here."

Inside, Lucy was busy collecting slate, chalk and a map book to put by the door, after Hoani had told her that the Ruru was back in the tree, though this time it seemed to be alone.

As the family were eating their dinner, the familiar scratching came at the back door. Hoani and Lucy smiled at each other as she rose to answer the call.

"Can we come?" Alice and Naku asked with excitement.

"They may get frightened if too many of us answer the door. You may watch from the window."

When Lucy opened the door, she was surprised to see a Roroa Kiwi standing at Oriel's side.

"Hello Oriel." Lucy greeted him as she knelt down and reached for the slate and chalk.

Kerwin was aware they were being watched, looked up to see three other humans looking at them through the window. He realised they couldn't harm him there, so turned to see what this human was doing.

"Are you wanting some more books?" Lucy asked. She wrote 'More Books?' on the slate, and 'Who is your friend?' and pushed it forward for Oriel and the kiwi to see.

Oriel pulled the slate to him. He tried to write,

but wasn't very skilled at it. He usually asked the possums to write letters on the slate for him in the classes and when he visited Amy.

"Do you want me to write for you?" Kerwin asked Oriel as he pulled the slate towards him and put his claw out for the chalk.

Kerwin looked at the words Lucy had written. He wrote 'Yes' and 'Kerwin' and pushed the slate towards Lucy.

Lucy pointed to the Kerwin on the slate and spoke "Kerwin." Before pointing at him and saying "Kerwin" again. Kerwin realised this human was saying his name. He looked into her eyes and saw the kindness there. He finally felt safe here. Lucy pulled the slate towards her, removed the words and wrote some more.

'Where do you want the books?' was passed back to them. Lucy then opened the atlas at the South Island and pushed it towards them.

Both Kerwin and Oriel leaned over the map to find Lake Kaniere. Oriel also spotted Mt Tuhua marked on the map.

"Tell her 'Top of Mount Tuhua.' Oriel advised Kerwin.

The slate had 'top ^ Tuhua' when passed back to Lucy. She looked at them both with incredulous eyes and looked up towards the top of the mountain, now cloaked in darkness.

"Up there?" Lucky pointed and looked before looking back at them. Oriel pulled the slate back for Kerwin to write 'Yes'.

'We will bring books up Tuhua.' Lucy wrote.

Lucy saw smiles on their faces as the Ruru

and kiwi looked at each other and her before they departed.

Lucy watched as Oriel flew off into the forest, while Kerwin padded down the steps to the garden. Instead of running off into the forest, he went over to the vegetable garden. As soon as he stood on the garden bed, he could feel worms – lots of them! Kerwin gave a call to Karamu, Kahuia, Kamahi, and Karri who were waiting on the edge of the forest.

The family joined him in having the best feed they had ever had. While they were feeding, Hoani Alice and Naku came to join Lucy to watch them. As they watched, they could hear other kiwi voices high on Tuhua's slopes. After the kiwi family retreated to the forest, Hoani and Lucy smiled at each other.

"It seems we have a Kiwi community living with us." Hoani spoke with excitement.

"I must tell mum!" Lucy exclaimed as she grabbed her phone.

Terry and Amy were settling in to a cosy evening by the fire in the front room when Lucy rang.

"Do you want me to leave Lizzie with Hori and Kohi?" Amy offered, though she knew that Lizzie was past chasing anything. The Labrador now spent most of her time resting and relaxing in her favourite places; either on the veranda in the sun or by the fire when it was damp and cold.

"She should be fine." Lucy reassured her. "Do you have any spare copies of books in the house to bring out? Oriel wants some for the top of Tuhua."

"How are we going to get them up there?" Amy

wanted to know.

"Have you got any backpacks?" Lucy asked. "I have a couple of smaller ones the children brought their toys and books in, if needed."

When Terry and his family arrived at the bach the next morning, two large back packs full of books came with them.

After Kerwin climbed to their burrow on the summit of Tuhua for their sleep, he started to dig another tunnel in their burrow.

"What are you doing?" Karamu asked.

"Making room for the books when they come."

When he had finished, Karamu had a pile of ferns waiting to line the tunnel.

Their sleep was interrupted that day. Daisy Duck also had been told that Terry and Hoani were climbing the mountain with backpacks on their backs.

When they reached the top, Terry and Hoani stopped for a much needed rest, and to enjoy the view. They were wondering where to leave the books when a duck came to land on a nearby branch, quacking at them. Both Hoani and Terry recognised it as one that visited the bach.

"We have your books." Terry said as he proceeded to open his backpack and showed the duck a book. Daisy then landed on the ground in front of them, moving to a tree closer to the burrow, waiting for them to follow. Near the burrow, Daisy made a loud call to Kerwin. This brought both Kerwin and Karamu outside.

'They have brought your books.' Daisy quacked.

When Hoani and Terry unloaded the books by the

burrow entrance, Kerwin was happy to see they were covered in plastic. It took time, but eventually the kiwis had the books stowed in their place.

That evening Kerwin was still tired after his interrupted sleep and extra activity to store the books, so a shorter session was had that night. Oregon was excited to see all the new books waiting in the burrow, was disappointed when his session finished early. After seeing the tiredness on Kerwin's face, he accepted that he would have to wait for the following evening to sneak a peek at his books. The spirit animals too wanted to see the books that had been brought here.

THE BOAT

Hoani and Lucy woke up early. Everyone else in the bach were still asleep. Hoani was feeling sore after the climb up Mount Tuhua, with the backpack full of books yesterday. A swim would be a good remedy to relieve the stiffness.

"Do you feel like a dip?" he whispered. Lucy's reply was a big smile as she leapt out to change. Grabbing their towels, they silently made their way to the front door. Terry grinned as he came out of his and Amy's room, giving them a little wave, and wishing that he could join them. He was feeling stiff as well. He might persuade Amy to go for one later.

Out in the main living area, Lizzy was in her basket, supervising the sleeping children on their lounge beds. She put her head up at the sound of footsteps coming down the passage. At the sight of Terry in the kitchen, she put her head down again. It wasn't time for the family to get up yet. Terry usually took her for a gentle stroll in the forest when they came out here, Emily and Jimmy running ahead to explore, under the canopy of the tree ferns. Alice and Naku would be joining them this morning.

As Hoani and Lucy walked down to the shore, the sky was clear, without a cloud in sight. The early morning sun peeping over Mount Tuhua. They usually swam to the jetty and back, but this morning, the Islands beckoned. Lucy saw Hoani's eyes on the Islands and let him take the lead.

She didn't notice till they were nearly at the small sand beach, that they had company on their swim. Several eels had made the swim with them. Lucy was reassured that they were swimming beside her, keeping her company, with no attempt to take any "nibbles" from her. Hoani was alarmed at first to look round to see the eels surrounding Lucy, but she was looking at them and smiling.

"You want to explore?" Hoani asked when Lucy joined him.

"I would love to! I've never been on here." Lucy replied as she followed Hoani onto the island.

As they meandered among the ferns and mossy floor under the leafy canopy above them, Hoani spotted something wooden hidden under some king ferns. He pulled it out to find a roughly hewn canoe. Some paddles fashioned from branches with flax woven between them, still inside.

"Some kids must have made it!" Hoani grinned at Lucy. "It's too narrow for an adult, which is a shame."

"I wonder why they left it?" Lucy was puzzled. "They must have swum back."

"Maybe it's not water-proof" Hoani commented as he took a good look at both the outside and inside of the boat, "though it looks intact."

"Are you going to test it on the way back?" Lucy asked. "The kids may like to play with it, though we will have to get some proper paddles."

As Hoani picked up the canoe to take it to the beach where they had arrived, the light filtering into the forest dimmed, and a breeze ruffled through the trees.

Lucy noticed that the eels were nearby when they returned to the beach. When Hoani launched the boat, pushing it ahead of him as he swam, some of the eels raced away, towards the shore, while others kept Lucy company while she swam. Soon a duck came to sit in the boat, quacking at Hoani as he pushed it towards the shore. He recognised it as the same one that led them to the kiwi burrow on Tuhua the day before.

"I would love to know what that duck is saying." Hoani commented to Lucy with amusement.

"I would love to know too!"

Back onshore, they dried off with their towels. The duck was still sitting in the boat. Hoani noticed that the inside of the boat was still completely dry. They didn't want to tip the duck out, so picked up each end of the canoe and gave the duck a ride back to the bach. Leaving the boat under the veranda at the back of the bach, they hung out their towels to dry, before joining the family for breakfast.

Wesley Weka saw Daisy Duck sitting in the boat as Hoani and Lucy brought it back to the bach. He waited till Hoani and Lucy went indoors before racing over to join Daisy as she hopped off the boat. Wesley had heard about the boat that had been left on the Island, and now it was here, with Daisy aboard.

"How did the humans know the boat was there?" Wesley asked Daisy.

"I think they found it. The eels came and told me the humans were bringing it back, so I sat in it to see what they did with it. I will have to let Oriel know it is here. Keep an eye on it, and let someone know if they take it anywhere."

By now Hovea Hedgehog had joined them.

"We will!" Hovea promised.

Her memory of the night that Oriel took the school for a trip to Dorothy Falls in the boat, came back to her as Hovea rubbed her paw along the boat. She remembered the frantic rush to reach the Islands as the sounds of the Moa and Harrier from the spirit world clashed behind them. Taking shelter in the big space under a big tree, before Kupe and Kaori Kiwi from the spirit world took all the animals for a flight to the school cave; but the harriers followed them there. Another flight took them to the community in the Arahura Valley till it was safe to return home again.

After Terry took Lizzie and the children for their walk in the forest, Hoani showed him the boat he had found. He looked at the branches woven with flax for paddles.

"We will definitely need some proper paddles!" Terry commented. He then turned the boat over to look at the outside. It had been left intact, which helped to keep it watertight. Looking at the inside, it needed to be smoothed to remove any splinters or jagged edges. Some seats would need to be put in as well.

"Someone did a good job on this," was Terry's verdict. "But we can certainly improve it and make it more stable. I will bring some paddles and timber out next weekend."

That evening, the bach received another visit. Amy and Lucy looked at each other with surprise. They didn't expect a request for more books so soon. This time, the possum was with Oriel. When Amy asked if they wanted more books, she wasn't ready for the reply.

'No. You have our boat.'

Amy turned her head towards the table where the family were sitting.

"The boat belongs to the animals. I will find out where they keep it."

'It is hidden by the water'

'Show us your hiding place. We will bring it back here for safety after you use it'

Oriel thought for a moment before agreeing. More humans had moved to the lake. It was possible other humans would find their boat and keep it. At least they still could use the boat with it kept at Amy's place. It was also dryer here too.

After Terry and Hoani worked on the boat, the animals found the inside was much smoother, there also was a floor in the boat and some new paddles were inside. Two pairs of wheels had been attached to the underneath and a rope had been attached to the front. They noticed that four seats were nearby.

Whenever Jimmy, Emily, Alice and Naku took the boat out, eels came to swim next to the boat. Daisy and her family also came to sit on the boat for the ride too.

As Terry Amy Hoani and Lucy watched them from the shore, they realised that they would need a bigger boat – one that they could use as well.

KORU

Koa dozed in the late afternoon light. Kewena was still asleep beside him. Their children Kehi and Koru along with Kio, who was now part of the family, had their own tunnels and entrances so they didn't disturb them as much.

He knew it would soon be time to return to their home in the Arahura Valley, though there was no hurry. Koa was surprised at how well his friend Kerwin and his community had settled here. He was grateful that Kamoku had also settled here. For on the occasions that Kerwin was on top of the mountain, giving Oregon his lessons, the community turned to Kamoku for advice. Even though Kamoku had no leadership ambitions for this community, everyone accepted his "ownership" of the area, given his family history here and Kamoku's vow to the harriers that he was here to reclaim his territory.

The sound of light footsteps passing their burrow entrance made Koa more alert. He smiled to see his daughter Koru carefully making her way to the school cave. He noticed her giving surreptitious glances around as she went. His interest aroused, Koa waited a minute or two before following her.

Koru had loved her stay at the lake. She wanted to live here, but wasn't sure whether her parents would allow it. She had made friends with the single females in the community who had offered to share their burrows with her. Koru now had another reason to stay. A certain book in the library was beckoning her to read it.

The school cave was empty as Koru skipped down the steps. Running across the floor of the cave, Koru took another look back at the entrance, though no-one was there. In the library corner, she looked up at the book, which was prominently displayed, but out of reach. If she moved the ladder next to it, she might be able to open it.

Koru had a feeling someone was watching, but again there was no sign of anyone around. Very carefully, Koru inched the ladder closer to the book, till she was satisfied she could reach it. Climbing the rungs, Koru didn't hear the quiet footsteps on the stairs.

Hanging on with one claw, Koru carefully reached out with her other claw to touch the book. She was about to lift the cover, when a voice behind her startled her.

"Are you sure you are ready to read that book?"

Koru's head swiftly swivelled around. Her father stood there, with a big grin on his face.

Koa had wondered whether his successor would be chosen before he moved to the spirit world. Here she was, just like his stepmother Kohana, who had hidden her attraction to the book.

"I am." Was Koru's simple but heartfelt reply.

"We will have to organise a ceremony." Another voice behind them made Koa turn around. A white kiwi was standing there, also with a big grin on his face.

"We certainly shall, Keoni!" Koa grinned back. He turned back to Koru. "There is much to teach you, before you read it." He looked at her quizzically. "You know what it means, don't you?"

Koru looked at her father with questioning eyes.

"What do you have to teach me?"

"About your Kingdom, of course. When I move to the spirit world, you will be the next Kiwi Kingdom leader. We will start your lessons tonight."

At Amy's bach, Hovea Hedgehog and Wesley Weka were startled to find a new family were settling themselves in, to live there. An older couple were caring for two children, who sat on the couch on the back veranda with them, cuddling the children in their arms as they wept.

Hovea and Wesley could only wonder what had happened to make the children so sad.

REVENGE!

Kiwa and Toro had a break from their lawnmowing round, by taking Toro's Ute to the Park at Blaketown Quay. Large waves broke over both the Blaketown and Cobden breakwater. The sea was a calmer now after the storm that raged overnight and into the morning. They watched in silence as a vessel from the fishing fleet made its way out over the turbulent waters of the Bar.

"You don't miss it?" Toro broke the silence after the boat navigated out to sea safely.

"No." Kiwa allowed himself a smile. After five years, and some counselling he was now able to remember the day he nearly lost his life on one of the fishing fleet boats without fear.

"If I want to fish, I will buy a tinnie and try my luck on the lakes."

"I will join you in that!"

They were eating their lunch when a car came and parked next to them. Toro didn't take much notice, untill Kiwa, who had also noticed the arrival frowned and commented

"It looks like someone is looking for you!"

As Toro swung round, two males were approaching his side of the Ute. The sight of them made Toro's heart sink.

He recognised them from his days in Auckland. These men were from a rival gang that had moved into the West Coast now that Kiwa's brother Ben and his gang had gone. Reluctantly, Toro put down his window.

"I've tee'd it with Kawa." The leader spoke without any preamble. "You are to become one of us, with the usual initiation, of course."

"No!" Toro was equally to the point. "I bought out of Kawa's gang when I married Mahina. I made it clear to Kawa I wasn't going to join any other gangs, so go and recruit elsewhere."

The leader was silent for a few moments.

"Don't be surprised if shots come your way."

"Do your worst! I'm not budging!"

With that Toro put up his window again. As the leader and his mate returned to their car and drove off, he made the comment.

"Well, we did try to protect and warn him!"

"Are you going to move?" Kiwa asked in alarm, after they had gone.

"We aren't going anywhere!" Toro's tone was final. "You know how futile "going on the run" is. They will find us no matter where we go." He turned to Kiwa.

"If they bump me off, can you take care of Mahina and the kids?"

"That's a given! From now on though, it will be best if we work together, instead of doing different rounds."

Toro doubted the wisdom of Kiwa putting himself in danger as well, but didn't object to having Kiwa near, now that he was vulnerable. Toro waited till the children were safely in bed before he gave Mahina the news.

"Are you sure you don't want to join the other gang?" Mahina asked. "At least you will have their protection if you join them." She knew though, that their life would change dramatically if he did join them.

"It's not happening!" Toro's tone was emphatic.

That night it took a long time for both of them to settle to sleep. Toro realised that he needed to get his affairs in order, just in case. An appointment with a solicitor was arranged, and money he had been saving for a holiday for the family to visit Auckland to see his whanau was put straight onto the mortgage. His priority now was to pay it off. Toro didn't want Mahina left with any debts.

In Kiwa and Reka's house they too were finding it difficult to get to sleep, after Kiwa told her of the gang's visit to Toro.

"It's Kawa, again; isn't it?" Reka asked with a sigh. "If Toro had gone into the gang, he would have had protection from them. As it is, he is a sitting duck!"

Kiwa nodded his agreement. "It looks like it. Toro is refusing to move. I'm not sure I would have his courage in this situation." Reka came to cuddle Kiwa as the families faced change in an uncertain future.

Toro had earphones on with his favourite music as he mowed the front lawn. Kiwa was out the back yard scooping up loose grass and leaves. Toro didn't see or hear the car draw up behind him. The first he knew was pain that shattered both his knees. As his body crumpled from the blow of the bullets, a third bullet struck Toro on the breast bone, before ricocheting up into his jaw.

The sound of rifle shots sent both Kiwa and the house owner racing out to the front, to find Toro lying unconscious and injured on the ground. The lawn mower was now mowing the neighbour's lawn. As Kiwa ran to stop the mower, he could see a dark car moving swiftly away down the road.

"He's been shot!" Mick the homeowner called in alarm.

"Have you anything to stop the bleeding? Towels will do!" Mick quickly ran inside to do Kiwa's bidding, returning with both towels and bandages to stem the bleeding from Toro's neck and knees. Kiwa was pleased to see that Toro was still breathing, even if he couldn't talk to him. Kiwa then removed the trailer from the tow-ball before opening the back door of the Ute.

"Help me get him in!" Kiwa called to Mick as he started to drag Toro across the grass to the Ute.

"You aren't waiting for an ambulance?"

"It will take too long!"

With an effort they bundled Toro into the back of the Ute. By now, other neighbours had come out to see what was going on.

"Call the hospital and tell them that gunshot wounds are coming in!"

By now, the police who had also heard the shots, were receiving calls about them. Cars were sent to all the exits from town to check everyone who was leaving. When the call came in that Toro the mower man had been shot at Micks and he was on his way to the hospital, an officer was also sent there. In the meantime, Kawa and his gang members headed towards the wharf area. In a side street they came to a dilapidated house with an old shed next to it. Kawa hopped out and opened the wooden doors for the driver. Within a few minutes the car was safely hidden from sight. After a phone call, they casually walked to their arranged meeting at the dock where a fishing boat was waiting. Kawa and his gang were swiftly ushered down below out of sight.

Mahina and Reka were supervising the children outside, when the sound of shots from a rifle rang out in the distance. They tried not to show their anxiety in front of the children. Mahina reached into her pocket for her phone to call Toro's number. There was no reply. Reka reached for her phone. There was no reply from Kiwa's phone either.

Mahina and Reka looked at each other with bleak eyes. The life that they had built and loved was about to change forever.

"Can you look after the children? I'm going to the hospital."

"Of course! Take care and call me when you have any news."

Mahina forced herself to be calm as she drove to the hospital. She saw Toro's Ute parked outside the emergency vehicles bay. Staff were crowded around the vehicle as they worked to transfer Toro to a trolley. Swiftly parking her car, Mahina ran back to the bay, but he had been taken inside. She then ran in to the ED reception.

"My husband Toro has just been brought in. He's been shot!"

"Please take a seat. I will let the medical team know you are here."

A couple of minutes later, the ward co-ordinator came out to take Mahina into the family room.

"Did someone call you to give you details?" the co-ordinator asked.

" No. I heard the shots. I tried to call Toro, but he didn't answer, so I knew it was him, so I came straight here."

The co-ordinator looked startled. "You were expecting it?"

"Yes."

Mahina explained how Toro had been part of a gang before they had married and that the local gang had tried to recruit him before warning that he could be shot.

"What is happening now?" Mahina asked with increasing anxiety. Why can't I see him?"

"The team is busy stabilising Toro. He has wounds to both knees, his chest and his jaw. He will then be transferred to Christchurch for treatment. You wish to go with him?"

"Of course."

"You have children?"

"They are being cared for."

"You will be called when Toro is stable."

"Thank you."

After the co-ordinator left, Mahina turned to her phone to message Reka. As she was texting, Kiwa came to join her. Wordlessly, he took Mahina in his arms to give her a hug.

"How is he?" Mahina tried to keep tears at bay but failed.

"Toro was already unconscious when I found him, so I bundled him into the Ute and brought him here."

"Thank you! They are taking Toro to

88

Christchurch when he is stable. I will be going with him."

"Of course! We will take care of everything here."

It was Mahina's turn to give Kiwa a hug. She finished and sent Reka's text before sending one to both Toro's and her own parents, which was answered by a brief "We are coming!"

Kiwa stayed with Mahina untill she was called to join Toro on his journey to Christchurch. She could see that Toro now had a swollen bruised jaw. His face drawn, now he was sedated. A nurse was accompanying them on the journey.

Strapped into her seat on the Helicopter, as it rose to cross the Alps, Mahina's mind was whirling. There was so much to think about and do. Toro's partnership with Kiwa and Her partnership with Reka may have to end. If Toro survived they would have to move. Mahina had no idea where they would go or what she would do. One thing she was sure of, if her brother Kawa came near her again, she would make sure she was ready for him!

THE SEARCH FOR THE GANG

The police sergeant at Greymouth was becoming anxious. It had been a couple of hours, since the shooting. There was no sign of the gang on any of the roads out of the coast. He hoped that they hadn't slipped through the surveillance that had been set up on the roads. It would be kept in place untill they knew where the culprits were.

For once police knew who they were searching for. The photos of Kawa and other gang members had been circulated to all police in the South Island. He had checked at the airport. No planes had left since the shooting and there weren't any expected movements there till tomorrow, when someone would be there to check all the passengers.

The sergeant had also checked with the port authority, there weren't any unusual movements of boats in the harbour. The only expected movements were of the fishing fleet, later that night.

It had occurred to the sergeant that the gang were still in town, lying low in someone's home. Officers were sent to the homes of all the gang members and their club house. The officers noticed that the local gang were more relaxed about the search than they usually were.

"We were expecting your visit." The gang leader replied when asked why they were so relaxed and co-operative. "We had tried to recruit and protect Toro, but he refused. How is he?"

"Not good. It's too early to say whether he will

survive or not. They will of course be up for murder if he doesn't. Is there anything you can tell us?"

"We are out of the loop on this one."

The leader wasn't going to divulge he knew of a certain trawler that was going to rendezvous with another vessel while out fishing tonight, that he had put Kawa in touch with the trawler's captain for the get-away.

After what seemed like many hours, Kawa and the gang could hear movement and voices up on deck. The throb of the diesel motor as it sprung into life reassured them. The gang found they had to hang on, while the boat bobbed about, as it went through the turbulence of the bar at the entrance of the river. Up in the wheelhouse, there were grins on the faces of the crew, knowing the discomfort of their passengers below.

The trawler dropped its nets as usual. On this occasion, working in the northern range of the fishing ground. While all the other trawlers steamed straight to lay their nets at their next position, the trawler headed north. A phone call for GPS co-ordinates allowed them to locate the yacht, which was now using its motor. Kawa and his gang were now on deck, grateful that the sea was relatively calm tonight. An inflatable dingy with the gang aboard was lowered over the side, between the boats, a long line attached to the dingy was flung across to the yacht. Once secured, Kawa and the gang then had to climb a rope ladder up onto the yacht. They were ushered below, where dinner and comfortable beds were waiting. The yacht turned around to make its way up the coast, its sails now taking full advantage of the breeze. The trawler returned to its nets, taking its catch in with all the other trawlers.

A couple of evenings later, the yacht quietly slipped into the marina at the yacht club in Auckland. It's passengers gave a generous tip before catching a taxi home. By then, the West Coast police had to admit that the gang had slipped through their net.

CHANGE FOR TAMA & RANGI

Tama followed his friend Toby out of the school gate to the car, where Toby's mother Rachael was waiting to take them home. When she dropped Tama off at the childcare centre and picked up her daughter Samantha, Rachael noticed that only Reka was present. She was looking strained.

Reka had rung her casual workers, hoping one could come in at short notice, but none of them were available this afternoon. She managed to book one to work for the next fortnight, with a view to a permanent position.

"What's the matter, Reka? Have you had a bad day?" Rachael asked sympathetically. Rachael sometimes found caring for her two children a challenge. She didn't know how Reka and Mahina managed the ten children in their care all day, every day.

Reka gave a smile that didn't reach her eyes.

"You haven't heard about the shooting? It was Mahina's Toro. She is at the hospital."

Rachael gasped with horror. She had heard about a shooting in the town on the radio, but there weren't any details yet of who and why.

"You are looking after them all on your own? Is there anything I can do?"

"I would love to accept your help, but the rules and regulations don't allow it, unless you have a police clearance and working with children card?" Reka asked hopefully.

Rachael shook her head regretfully. "What are you going to do?"

"I have help for the next fortnight. We will hopefully know how to plan for the future by then."

Just then Tama came running out of the centre. He had a painting he had made in art class to show his mother.

"Where's Mum?" Tama asked, as he ran up to Reka.

Rachael moved away to leave, but Reka stopped her. "Not yet."

Reka knelt down to be at Tama's level and put her arm around him. He could see her face was serious, so he knew that something had happened.

"Tama, you and Rangi are staying here with us tonight. Your dad has been hurt. Your mum is at the hospital to be with him."

"Can we go to the hospital to see him?" Tama asked anxiously.

"No. Your dad is being taken to Christchurch for treatment. Your Mum is going with him. Your grandparents are coming down to care for you." Reka took a big breath before continuing. "You need to say goodbye to Toby, as you will be moving from Greymouth once your grandparents come. It may be a while before you see Toby again." Reka looked at Rachael. "Unless an arrangement can be made for you to see each other, maybe on the weekends?"

Rachael nodded her agreement. "You have my number."

By now Tama was starting to cry. His parents

were gone and now he was being taken from his friend as well.

"Can I have your painting, seeing you can't give it to your mum?" Toby asked, as he put his arm around his friend and gave him a hug. He was really going to miss him, and wondered whether he could find another friend at school as nice as Tama was. "Remember, we will see each other on the weekend!" Toby turned to his mother. "Can I stay with Tama this weekend?"

"It should be fine. We will make arrangements closer to the weekend." Rachael gave a little sigh.

"Why can't I go to school tomorrow?" Tama's anxiety was growing. He loved being in the class, being read stories and playing with his friends.

It was Reka's turn to sigh. "Your teacher is coming around later this evening to show me what lessons you need for the next couple of weeks. You won't be going to school because your grandparents will be taking you to your new home when they arrive."

"Where will our new home be? Tama wanted to know.

"It will be in the country, where there is lots of bush for you to explore and play in."

Three year old Rangi was confused when neither Mum or Dad came to take them home that night, but was happy to stay and play with Kiwa and Reka's children, Kohi and Moana.

Tama's teacher gave him a special smile when she came in to see Reka, showing the her the lessons that were expected to be completed in the coming weeks, with suggestions for activities for learning and play. She advised she would visit him in a week to see how he was progressing.

Before Tama and Rangi went to bed that night, Reka made a video call to Mahina. She was waiting in the visitors room. Toro was in theatre having his knees attended to. He would have another session in theatre, in a few days when the swelling in his jaw reduced.

Tama and Rangi had to make do with kissing the phone screen and waving goodnight to their mother. Tama felt a little better that he was able to see mum on the screen, but he was still missing his dad terribly. Reka and Kiwa made sure both Tama and Rangi had lots of cuddles when they were settled to sleep for the night. Tama had his own room, while Rangi was given a mattress in with Kohi and Moana.

The next morning, Tama joined Rangi and the other children at the childcare centre. He was given some paints to make some pictures and some play dough to make some animals. Hearing voices, Tama looked up. His grandparents from Auckland were here!

"Nan! Grandad!" Tama called out as they came into the room. He ran into their arms.

"Hello Tama Love! We are here to look after you while Dad is in hospital. His grandfather said as he gave him a big cuddle. Rangi also came for a cuddle too.

"Will you be taking us to see Dad?" Tama wanted to know.

"Your Dad is too sick for us to visit. We will have to wait till he is better."

In Christchurch, Toro's parents had joined Mahina at his bedside. Toro was still sedated to protect him from the shock his body had received. Both of his knees had been replaced. His broken jaw was still swollen and bruising made a black shadow on his face. His chest wound had also been dressed.

They had hours of discussions on what would be the best path for the family for the future. Mahina knew that even if Kawa was caught, he would enlist someone from another gang to finish what he had started. It was going to be difficult to protect Toro and their family while having a normal life.

Mahina already accepted that she would have to find some other form of employment. Even if Toro continued with the upholstery business, it wouldn't be enough to keep them comfortably. Their home would also have to be sold too. Finding a place where they could be safe, but with access to school for the children was going to be a challenge.

Reka had called to say that her parents had arrived to care for the children. They would be staying at Amy's bach for now. When Mahina mentioned that their home would be sold, Reka told her not to worry, they would look after it till she was ready to list it.

Mahina had a bitter/sweet talk to her parents and to the children before she had to leave the room while the staff attended to Toro.

Tama had a glimpse of his father in the background. He was still asleep, with lots of tubes and lines attached to his body. It was only then that he realised how ill his father was and that he might not come back to them.

For the rest of the day, Tama was unusually quiet.

Rangi noticed it. She had no idea why Tama was sad, but she came to give him a cuddle. He clung to her for several minutes.

"I'm worried about Dad." Was all he said, but Rangi understood. She was missing him and worried about him too. Even though she didn't understand what had happened. Mahina's parents were out collecting supplies for their stay at the bach and collected clothes and toys for the children from their home. Reka had been busy with other children, missed the exchange between them.

When the children were eventually packed into the car, Tama wanted to know why they were going to the country instead of going home.

Mahina's parents looked at each other. They didn't want to frighten them with the truth.

"It's easier for us to look after you there. Your dad will be needing a place that is quiet and peaceful to recover, when he gets out of hospital"

When Mahina's parents drew up at the Bach, Amy was there to welcome them, giving them a hug. Before showing them where everything was.

Tama looked around. They were surrounded by thick forest. Mount Tuhua loomed overhead. Apart from Amy, there wasn't anyone else around, including children. There were no shops here either. He did spot the lake down the hill. Tama realised then, that they were hiding here. He wondered what the danger was.

Tama went out the back veranda to sit on the couch, lost in his own thoughts. Rangi came and sat with him and held Tama's hand. Mahina's parents were unpacking groceries in the kitchen when her mother spotted them.

"We can do this later." They both went out to sit on the couch to give them a cuddle. They could see the tears welling in Tama's eyes.

"Will we ever go back to our house?" Tama wanted to know.

Mahina's mother gave an inward sigh. They needed the truth.

"Probably not. It is going to be sold. Your mum and dad will be looking for a home somewhere else."

"What about all of our things?"

"They will be coming to you or put in storage untill you move to your new home. When your dad comes home, you will be starting a new life."

The grandparents held them close while the tears flowed. Rangi also understood that they wouldn't be going home again ever.

RESCUING TORO

Toro woke with someone calling his name and telling him to wake up. When he opened his eyes, he was surrounded by strangers. Mahina was there too. Although she was smiling, there were tears in her eyes.

When Toro tried to sit up, his head spun and his jaw hurt. His knees felt heavy too! Then he remembered! He had been shot!

"Take is easy!" the doctor spoke as he gently pushed Toro back down onto his pillow. "You've been through a lot and you have some work to do before you get back onto your feet. Do you remember what happened?"

Toro nodded. He wasn't sure he trusted his voice. His first attempt to speak produced a croak, so he cleared his throat and tried again.

"I shouldn't be here!" He looked at Mahina with troubled eyes. "What are we going to do?"

Mahina squeezed Toro's hand. His other hand had a drip with a white liquid – Total Parental Nutrition, which Toro was to learn was to be his "food" untill he was able to eat again. Even then, he was to have soft "baby food" untill his jaw had healed. It now contained metal rods to hold it together.

"You are safe here." Mahina reassured Toro. "Just concentrate on getting better. There is plenty of time to sort out our future."

However, when Mahina left the ICU unit to grab some lunch, two men were waiting for her outside the doors. She knew immediately they were from the local gang.

"How is he?" one of them asked.

Mahina ignored the question, glaring at them.

"So you've got your orders to finish him off, already!"

She stalked off; a resolute expression on her face.

They looked at her receding back with admiration. Anyone else would be full of fear. It occurred to Mahina, that she and the children were now in danger too.

As she ate her lunch, oblivious to everyone around her, Mahina realised that as soon as Toro left ICU, they would be fair game. She would have to find a way of getting him out of the hospital. Rehab would have to be done at home. Finding out when the medical team planned to move Toro and the schedule of rehab was needed too.

Mahina's thoughts were interrupted by the arrival of Toro's Parents.

"You were looking thoughtful!" Toro's father greeted her.   Mahina managed to smile.

"I have plenty to think about." Her voice and expression was now serious.

"I have good news! Toro is awake. The not so good news, is that the local gang is hanging around the ICU already. It can only mean they have their orders to kill him." She paused, "and us as well." Mahina nodded her head at the stricken look on his parents' faces. "We have to find a way to smuggle him out. Rehab will have to be at home. Where is your car parked?"

"In the car park."

Back at the ICU, Toro's parents sat at Toro's side while Mahina had a chat with the co-ordinator. She found that the plan was to move him to the orthopaedic ward the following morning. The speech therapist was going to check Toro's ability to swallow puree food and drink fluids this afternoon, along with a visit by the physio to see how Toro could stand and take steps. Mahina didn't tell her of the danger to Toro or her plans to remove him.

After the speech therapist had been and cleared Toro to take Puree food, Toro was happy to have his drip removed. The Physio then came with some crutches. Before he attempted to get up, the physio put him through his paces with some exercises on the bed. Mahina was pleased to see she left a sheet of exercises for him to do. Toro felt light-headed when he sat on the side, but it wasn't as strong as the first time he sat up. He waited a minute or so before attempting to stand. To Toro's amazement his legs felt normal to stand on and there was no pain. Carefully with the use of crutches, Toro walked around the bed to sit in the chair placed next to it. After a few minutes, he felt tired and was ready for a rest on the bed.

"You have done so well!" Mahina gave Toro a kiss after he was comfortable on the bed again. "Have a rest and we will be back later."

Mahina's father dropped Mahina and her mother off at the motel where they had been staying, while he went off to fill the tank with petrol. As Mahina was bringing her bag out, to put in the boot, the door of the next motel unit opened. It was one of the gang members who had been at the hospital.

"Leaving already? He asked.

"Of course not!" Mahina retorted. "We are just moving in with some rellies, as Toro will be going to rehab soon."

There was silence as they drove away from the motel. "What is your plan?" Toro's father wanted to know. He could see they were being followed.

"I am going to rent a van, so there is room for Toro to lie down. When you drop off the car, we will separate. You look for a bus that is heading in to the hospital. I will bring the van to the car park. I will be dressed as a man, so they won't immediately know it is me. I will meet you outside ICU."

After collecting the keys and putting her bag in the van, Mahina slipped into the ladies to change. Jeans, a large jacket turned up, her hair style changed under a baseball cap, sunglasses and a moustache, along with walking a different gait, transformed Mahina's appearance. When Mahina drove out of the car hire firm, she headed away from the city, ignoring the car sitting on the other side of the road. She drove several blocks before making a turn. Checking in her mirror, the gang were still sitting outside the car hire firm.

Knowing that the gang would check the visitors car park, Mahina found a parking bay near the laundry, before making her way to the ICU unit.

"They were still sitting outside the car hire firm when I left." Mahina smiled at Toro's anxious parents.

"He's just gone down for an Xray." Toro's father

Informed her.

"Good! This is our chance." Mahina said as she led the way to the Xray department, where Toro was sitting in a wheelchair. He gave them a grin as he was taken through to the Xray room.

When he returned, Mahina waited till the staff left the room. She noticed a desk with an out tray, leaving a sealed envelope with "For ICU" on it. Mahina then wheeled Toro out of the Xray department, leading his parents to the laundry area. Between them they helped Toro into the van, with the wheelchair and crutches. Toro's parents sat in the back with Toro. Mahina put her disguise back on before driving out of the laundry area, heading out Riccarton Road for the West Coast.

By the time the gang realised and checked that Mahina was no longer at the car firm, the van had already departed from the hospital. When the staff at ICU made enquiries whether Toro's Xray had been done yet, the van was well into the Arthurs Pass. Then the letter Mahina had left at the Xray department arrived.

The staff were going to call the police, but after reading that Toro would be killed if he remained in the hospital; also the family took full responsibility for the premature discharge of Toro from hospital care, and his discharge against medical advice. The letter was added to Toro's file which was closed.

When darkness fell, Mahina took the cap moustache and sunglasses off. She had half expected a police car to stop them, but none came. At Arthurs Pass they stopped for a quick break. All the shops were shut, so they pressed on. Mahina now had to take extra care on the road as rain had set in. At Kumara Junction, they turned right for Greymouth and the Supermarket.

Mahina sent her parents in with a shopping list, which included baby food, pain relief and some dressings for Toro, who was now sitting with his legs up on the seat. They would have liked to stop at Kiwa and Reka's place, but didn't in case it was being watched. Keeping to back streets, they made their way south. It was with great relief that they drew up at the bach.

The front veranda light came on, then Mahina's Father came out. When Mahina waved, he shot back in, reappearing with her mother and the children, who were jumping up and down to see Mum was back. Two large golf umbrellas were brought out to shelter everyone as they emerged from the van.

They were stunned to see Toro emerge, still in his hospital gown and on crutches. Toro hadn't had time to learn how to negotiate stairs with crutches, but after a couple of false starts, made it up onto the veranda and to the safety of indoors.

Much later, after cuddles with the children, some food and a much needed shower, where his knees and chest were covered in some plastic bags to keep his wounds dry, Toro enjoyed the comfort of a normal bed with Mahina, something he hadn't expected. From now on he would appreciate every day that he lived.

Reka was ready for bed when she received a text from Mahina. "Safe with the children."

NEW LIFE FOR THE FAMILY

Toro sat out on the back veranda of the bach, supervising Tama's school lessons and keeping an eye on Rangi as she played "tea party" with her toys. Both Parents had gone home. Mahina was out putting leaflets in the mail boxes of homes at the lake where she knew people with children lived, offering home care for children.

There were times when Toro struggled with the pain in his knees and jaw, but grit his teeth and put ice packs on when the Panadol and anti-inflammatory wasn't enough to keep him pain free after his exercises.

In their spare time, Kiwa and Reka were working on Toro and Mahina's home in Greymouth, tidying up the garden and preparing the inside for viewers. The Children's swing set was living at Hoani and Lucy's home for now. All the furniture and possessions that wasn't needed for display was now in storage, the walls getting a fresh coat of paint, floors scrubbed and the carpets cleaned. The real estate agent had been informed. He had people on his books looking for properties like theirs.

Toro wondered what he was going to do next. A job involving contact with the public was out of the question, but he didn't relish being on a computer all day every day, besides, he didn't think the internet reception out here was good enough for commercial needs.

He thought about things he could make. Carving jade appealed, but he didn't have the equipment he needed to grind and polish the stone into shape. Also the shed in the back yard was too small for the saws and polishing machines he would need. Then Toro saw a branch from the tree lying on the ground. Carving wood was much easier and quicker than stone. He didn't have to worry about running out of branches around here. He asked Tama to bring the branch to him.

Tama was immediately more interested in what his father was going to do with the branch than his lessons, but he was told he needed to learn his lessons before learning about carving. They would do it later after his lessons, if he could find the right tools.

Kiwa gave his mate Mike from his days at Manapouri a call, asking him to call in and see how Toro was going. Mike's home was just up the road from Amy's bach. His wife Anne was going to have their second child soon.

When Mahina arrived back from dropping her leaflets, Toro had a shopping list of tools he wanted from the hardware shop, which was messaged through to Kiwa.

It was late afternoon when a knock came at the front door of the bach. Mike and Anne with two year old Ash were on the doorstep. She had brought a plate of nibbles. Mahina was in the process of preparing veges for dinner. A few more were added to the pot. Anne had worked untill Ash was born and had managed casual work till now, was happy to learn she had a childminder on her doorstep and arranged for Mahina to care for Ash when she needed to work. Once their next child was settled, they would be coming for care as well.

In coming days another three preschool children and a couple of other school age children would come for after school care.

Mahina was able to arrange for Tama to be given a lift to school at Kaniere with other children at the lake. At first Tama found it strange that the different grades were in the same room, but he soon made friends and enjoyed the extra attention he was given to help him catch up with his lessons.

During Mike and Anne's visit, Mahina enquired whether there was a firing range near Hokitika, as she wanted to try it out. Mike raised his eyebrows, as the last time there was shooting, he and his mates had to move on from Manapouri.

"What's up?" Mike asked. "Is someone after you?"

Mahina looked at Mike with serious eyes as she nodded. "Do you remember when Reka was kidnapped and brought down south to be killed with Kiwa?"

"Who could forget that!?" Mike shook his head.

"Well, I was kidnapped with her. Our kidnapper was my brother, Kawa. Toro was in the gang at the time, but when we married, he bought out of it. The trouble now, is Kawa has put the word out for us to be killed. I want to be able to defend us, both with arms and self-defence."

Mike was thoughtful. "There is a rifle range over at Kowhitirangi. Daniel and Cheryl in Greymouth would be the best people to teach you self-defence, though I can teach you a few moves to get you out of a tight spot."

"Thank you Mike. Greymouth is a little too public. I don't want the gang there following me home. It is very difficult for us at present, having to keep a low profile. Shopping is out of the question and we are having to rely on Kiwa and Reka to prepare our home in Greymouth for sale."

"Where will you settle?" Mike wanted to know.

"We love our life here. We are looking for a bach, or a section for sale so we can build. We are lucky there is no time limit on our stay here."

"How many bedrooms?"

"Four to five." Mahina grinned at Mike's raised eyebrow. "We need four for us!" She patted her still flat stomach. "Plus a guest bedroom. We also are looking for space for my childcare business and Toro's workshop for his carving."

"It sounds like you need a larger version of our house! Tomorrow, you come to our place for drinks and dinner!"

The next evening, they wandered up to Mike and Anne's house. It was a slow journey for Toro on his crutches, and the challenge of the climb up the stairs to the living area. Both Toro and Mahina made a mental note to put a lift in their house. They were glad it was a fine evening, to enjoy the views from the living area and the deck.

Both Toro and Mahina could see that with some tweaking, this house plan would suit them very well. They also were impressed with the space on the ground floor, that gave them room for parking as well as Toro's workshop and Mahina's Childcare centre.

Mike showed them the website where they bought their home. On there, they found a plan that suited them perfectly. It would depend on the price they received for their home how many fixtures and fittings they started with.

HUNTED

Toro was out in the back yard, checking the garden. Mahina had taken the children indoors to give them some fruit and read them a story. Suddenly he heard in the distance the sound of a drone. Toro knew he was too far from the house to climb back up the veranda, so he moved as quickly as he could to shelter under the tree, behind the shed, making sure he couldn't be seen from the air.

Inside the house, Mahina saw Toro look into the air, then rushed to the tree behind the shed. As the children were finishing their fruit, she quickly drew the curtains in the living area, making it dark. Mahina smiled at the children as she drew the curtains.

"I am going to tell you a ghost story! Who likes spooky stories? If you are afraid, you can hold my hand."

Immediately, a couple of hands came to cling to her arm. As Mahina told her story about a lost little ghost, she could hear the drone outside, checking all around the house, before moving on to another property. It gave her some satisfaction to hear one of the neighbours in the distance, give a roar of displeasure, telling the drone operator to "f... off!" and that he would smash the machine if he could get his hands on it!

Mahina realised that the gang must have some information that they were in this area. She definitely needed to implement her plan to protect her family. Once it was quiet again, Toro came indoors. Mahina gave him a cuddle.

"That was close." Mahina said.

Toro nodded. He hoped they wouldn't return. He didn't fancy having to live indoors all the time. While the children were having their afternoon nap, Mahina went online to find the rifle range at Kowhitirangi. They welcomed new members and had a competition day the coming Saturday. Mahina registered her details. She also messaged Mike that she needed those self-defence lessons he was going to give her.

When Mike came home, he came straight down, and took Mahina outside.

"The first thing you have to learn, is how to fall without hurting yourself, though what about the baby?"

"I can always have another one if I lose it." Mahina said firmly.

By the end of the session, Mahina not only mastered the technique of falling, but also learnt how to disarm someone who was attacking her.

That Saturday, Toro stayed at home to care for the children. Tama's friend Toby was also here for the weekend.

Mahina noticed that it was mainly men in the competition, that most of the ladies were there to provide the afternoon tea.

Mahina tried her hand at the clay pigeon competition, and was happy she managed to hit a couple of the targets. She also tried pistol shooting at the target, and was pleased she managed to hit the outer circle.

"There's plenty of room for improvement!" Mahina grinned at her tutor. "I can see I will have to strengthen the muscles in my wrists! I had no idea how heavy pistols could be."

"So you're coming back for another go?"

"Definitely! When is the next session? I will bring a plate next time."

"We have them weekly if you're keen. Are you planning on using your own weapon?"

"Not as this stage. I don't have a safe place to store it. Also I will need the necessary licence to keep one."

"Good girl!" the tutor approved. "Most people just go out and order weapons without any consideration of the risks and responsibilities that go with owning them."

Over the coming weeks, Mahina's Saturday afternoons were spent at the rifle range. One weekend they had a family day, so Toro brought the children along. By now Toro could walk without his crutches, though for only short distances. When Toro was offered a try, at first he refused. This brought back too many memories of his previous life, that he would prefer to forget.

He was persuaded to try the clay pigeon shoot and struck every target that was pulled.

"You've done this before!" the comment was made.

"Not Clay shooting, but yes, I have been around guns before."

"What doing?"

"I was in a gang."

"Enough said. You aren't interested in target shooting with pistols?"

"No. It brings back memories I would rather forget."

"Would you join our team for the Clay shooting?"

Toro sighed. "I won't be coming regular. There is a bullet out there with my name on it." Toro pointed at his knees and jaw. "They won't miss the next time."

The club member looked at Toro with concern.

"It was you that was shot in Greymouth?"

"Yeah. I bought out of the gang, but they won't stop till we are dead."

Why? What have you done for that."

"I haven't. It's usual gang policy that once you're in, you never leave, unless it's to go to another gang who give you their protection." Toro grinned at the club member. "I know I'm a sitting duck, but I prefer it, to having to put the gang before my family, not to mention the crime we are expected to commit and the long stretches away from the family while we do jail time."

The next week while Mahina was competing in the pistol shooting, she noticed that some men were standing at the fence. She recognised them as members of the gang at Greymouth. One of them had binoculars trained on the activity at the club.

"Excuse me, I need to have a word with those men!" Mahina spoke to the organiser. "I recognise them as the gang at Greymouth. They are looking for me."

"Don't get too close! If you approach them in a direct line from the clubhouse door, we will cover you with our rifles."

Activities stopped while Mahina made her way towards the fence. She still had her pistol in her hand.

The gang watched her approach to them, wondered what she had to say.

"Keep your guns in your pockets!" the gang member with the binoculars warned them. "Every rifle in the club is trained on us!"

At twenty metres away, Mahina stopped, a neutral expression on her face.

"I have a message for Kawa." She spoke loudly and firmly. "If anything at all happens to me or my family, I have arranged for Kawa and his family to be wiped out too. And, if any drones come anywhere near my home, I will shoot it out of the sky. Is that clear?"

There was a nod before the gang turned to leave. Mahina slowly withdrew, making sure she didn't turn her back on them, though the rifles trained their way, made sure Mahina stayed safe. Mahina realised that if the gang had followed her here, they must know where she and Toro were living. She was now wishing she had a pistol. She also needed much more practice with a pistol. The thoughts swirling through her head must have shown on Mahina's face.

"What did they say?" the organiser wanted to know when she reached the clubhouse.

"They didn't say anything, except that they understood my message to Kawa, and that any drones near my home would be destroyed." She took a large breath. "I need lots of practice with the pistol before I go home."

The organiser took Mahina round the back of the club house to a pistol gallery. He put a large box of ammunition next to her.

"Do you want the target or this?" He pulled a lever. The target was replaced by the figure of a man holding a gun.

"This will be good, thank you!"

Mahina started by aiming at the chest, then the head, body shots then the hand with the gun. She tried it again, standing side on, and withdrawing from her back pocket. Mahina then challenged herself by shooting with her other hand. She had nearly finished the box of ammunition, before she was satisfied she could manage using either arm if necessary.

As Mahina emptied the pistol and made sure it was safe, a round of applause came from behind her. She hadn't realised that she had an audience! All the ladies and some of the men were all peering over her shoulder at the target.

The organiser came forward. "Do you have somewhere safe to lock that pistol at home?"

Mahina thought of the cupboards in the laundry, which had locks.

"I do."

The organiser gave her a clip for ammunition. "Fill this and keep it separate to your pistol. I have a form for your weapon licence for you to fill in too. You can expect a visit from the police to check that your weapon is safe."

"Thank you so much." Mahina expressed her gratitude to the organiser before she left.

He patted her shoulder. "Let me say I'm happier that the odds against you are now evened up a little."

When Mahina arrived home, Toro had a look of

relief on his face.

"Did you know that you were followed to the club? It looked like the gang from Grey."

"No, but they made their presence felt by coming to the fence and using binoculars to see what I was doing, so I went over to have a little chat to them." Mahina saw Toro's look of alarm. "It was okay. All the members had their rifles trained on them, so they behaved. They shouldn't bother us here again. I sent a message to Kawa that if anything happens to us, that I have arranged for him and his family to be eliminated too."

"I've got some good news too!" Toro showed his elation. "The sale on our house in Greymouth has gone through and there is a section available here for us to build on. We will have to go in to town next week to make an offer on the section."

CONFRONTATION

The police came into the laundry and frowned as Mahina took the keys from around her neck to unlock the cupboards.

"They look like they could be ripped off the wall. I don't think they are a safe place for your weapon."

"You can try, if you like. You will have to take the wall as well."

Both police officers gave some vigorous tugs and pulls at the cupboards, but all of their efforts were futile. The cupboards didn't budge an inch.

"Okay it passes the security test. Let us see how you are storing it."

After seeing the gun had been dismantled and stored in separate cupboards, with the ammunition in a separate cupboard to the gun pieces, they were satisfied and signed off on her permit.

When the police left, Mahina noticed that a dark car followed the police car. The tinted windows didn't allow her to see the occupants. Mahina would have been alarmed if she could, for Kawa and his gang were back on the coast.

When it was time to travel into town, Mahina quietly loaded her pistol, and placed it in the back pocket of her jeans. Her thick woolly jumper covered it from view.

After visiting the agent to put a deposit on the section, they visited the supermarket. Mahina took her trolley of groceries through the checkout while Toro supervised the children as they picked out a book and toy each. In the glass entrance, Mahina stopped to look at some plants for sale, which she liked for their future home.

The whistle of two bullets right next to her ear as she bent over, followed by the familiar cracking sound of a pistol, told Mahina that she was being attacked. She was now very glad of the practice session at the rifle range. Swiftly Mahina pulled her pistol out of her pocket and returned fire at the figure running towards her from the doorway. As he dropped, another came into view directly behind him. He too was dropped with a headshot.

Mahina glance into the supermarket to see where Toro and the children were, but the sound of broken glass along with more shots came her way. As she looked back, Kawa and two other men were standing there. One of the shots hit her in the shoulder, the force of it sending her to the ground. More shots rained on Mahina as she fell. She could feel them hitting her body as she tried to protect herself. Mahina was now glad she had training on how to fall without hurting herself. Knowing she couldn't use that arm; Mahina switched the gun to her other arm and fired three quick shots at the men as she landed on the floor. For several seconds there was silence after Mahina fired, though she could hear the sound of running footsteps and shouting. She saw a figure in the doorway. It was Kawa. Before either Kawa or Mahina could aim their weapons, a much larger bang from a rifle sent his gun flying, as the bullet passed through his hand. Before he could chase after his gun, another bullet smashed into his thigh, sending him slumping to the floor. Mahina couldn't see him, but a deer stalker who happened to be in the car park, had seen the gang approach the supermarket with their pistols, was covering Kawa with his rifle till the police arrived. When the police came running in, Mahina put her pistol on the floor.

"Can you make it safe?" Mahina asked. "I have only one hand I can use at the moment." She attempted to sit up with her good hand.

The officer quickly put on gloves to empty the gun and placed it in a plastic bag.

"Where have you been hurt?" he asked.

"In my arm. I think there may be some in my leg too."

"MAHINA!! Are you alright?" Toro and the children came rushing out, along with the supermarket manager, who was stunned to see all the bodies and broken glass around.

"I think so, though I'm going to be a 'one-armed bandit' for a little while. I've been pinged in the arm and leg."

"You will be going to hospital for a proper check." The officer spoke. "Do you have a licence for this?" He held up Mahina's pistol.

"I do, though I don't expect to be using it for a while."

"In that case, we will hold it at the station for you. Just bring in your licence when you are ready to collect it. We want your account of what happened here too."

The officer looked at the manager. "We want the

footage from your camera too, please."

Mahina wasn't sure whether it was the loss of blood or the shock of the assault. "I'm not feeling so good." She said before she fainted.

When Mahina came round, she was in the ambulance, on the way to Greymouth Hospital. A drip with intravenous fluids had been inserted into her arm and her wounds had been dressed. She didn't ask what was happening to Kawa, though he too was being conveyed to hospital, in Christchurch – by helicopter, with a police escort. His smashed hand and injury to his thigh needed specialist care.

When Mahina told the medical team she was pregnant, a heavy lead-lined jacket was placed over her for the Xray to check on the location of the bullets. She was put under twilight sedation for the repair of her wounds. Toro and the children spent the afternoon with Kiwa and Reka while she was being attended to.

Once she was awake and comfortable, a woman police constable came to take a statement from Mahina.

"We've seen the footage of the incident." She said. "How you survived the shooting we don't know. That was some sharp shooting you did yourself. Where did you do your training?"

Mahina was able to smile. "I'm a member of the rifle club at Kowhitirangi. I had a visit from the gang in Greymouth on the weekend while at the club, so I made sure I practiced before I went home."

"Do you want a restraining order put on them?"

"Yes please."

When Reka heard of Mahina's plight, she asked

for one of her carers to help Mahina till she was able to care for the children herself. The carer jumped at the chance to have a "holiday" at Lake Kaniere and be paid while she was there.

A frantic phone call came from Mahina's parents, who had to be reassured that she would be okay and that Toro was well enough to care for everyone while she was recovering. Toro told them about the land they were buying and the house they were building. They promised to come down when the house was ready for visitors.

A couple of weeks later Mahina received a phone call. It was Noah, the leader of another gang in Auckland. His sister Pua was married to Kawa.

"How are you?" He asked.

"I'm sure you aren't calling about my health!" Mahina chose to be blunt. "What's up?"

Mahina detected a smile in Noah's voice as he replied. "I'm ending this family feud between you two!"

"Really?"

Noah ignored the disbelief in Mahina's voice.

"Yes. Your promise to wipe out Kawa's family meant that I had to get involved. Kawa is the only survivor of your shooting skills. We now have four families wanting justice. Given that Kawa started this, he knows he has to pay. Kawa is expected to get ten years inside, but he already knows he won't be coming out. He just doesn't know how or when. I have taken over his patch and am advising you, that you won't be bothered again."

"Good."

Toro saw Mahina's pensive mood after the phone call. He came to give her a hug.

"Is everything okay?"

Mahina was able to give him a reassuring smile.

"We are finally completely safe, though it comes at a price."

"What's that?"

"At some point in the future Kawa is to be eliminated. I know what he did to us, but he is still my brother."

NEW BEGINNINGS

When Mahina and Toro visited the rifle club, she still had her arm in a sling and was using an elbow crutch to walk. After receiving congratulations on her performance at the supermarket, Mahina was asked if she wanted to join in the pistol target competition. Mahina grinned, but declined.

"When I lose these crutches and sling, I will. Toro has decided to join the team in the clay pigeon competition."

Kiwa and Reka came down for a visit. They were given a look at the section of land that Toro and Mahina were going to build on, and the plan of the house that was going on it. It was just waiting for council approval.

Kiwa asked if Toro was interested in joining him with his mowing round again. There was too much work for him alone and the help he had employed hadn't lasted. It was arranged that once Mahina was fully back on deck, he would rejoin him.

Kiwa also mentioned that people were asking if Toro was still restoring furniture as they had items they wanted recovering.

Toro realised that this would take financial pressure off Mahina while she was recovering.

"You can tell them I am back in business, and I will put an ad in the paper." Toro promised.

"You will be wanting a house in Grey again!" Kiwa joked.

"No." Toro was firm. We love it out here. I don't

mind the drive to work. I can reduce time by cutting through Blue Spur to Arahura instead of going into town."

Reka was missing Mahina at the day care centre. She would have loved to ask her to come back to work with her, but she could see that Mahina was filling a need here.

"We will have to have a regular catch up," Reka suggested, now that you're staying here."

It was arranged that they would come down for lunch on Sundays. On the weekends that Amy and Lucy's family came out, the bach was overflowing, but no-one cared! – The more the merrier.

Early one morning, Mahina had to wake Toro. Strong contractions told her that she was in labour. By the time they dropped the children off with Reka and reached the labour ward, Taiko was ready to be born.

The day finally came when Toro and Mahina received the keys to their new home. Showers of rain mixed with sunshine. They were glad of the carport and veranda to keep dry. At the downstairs entrance, they stepped into the lift with boxes at their feet, to ride up to the entrance to the living area. Stepping into the large area which combined the kitchen with dining and living, they looked out through the bank of floor to ceiling windows and doors to the deck and the forest below. Beyond they could see the lake and Conical hill.

They gave each other a cuddle.

"I think there's enough room for us all in here." Toro commented.

"Yes." Mahina agreed. "It's good to be home."

JIMMY'S PROMISE

Amy and Terry were taking the children over to Christchurch for a visit. The favourite part of the trip was coming up for Jimmy. Whenever they drove over Arthur's Pass, they always stopped at the shop where they were born. The shopkeeper always made a fuss of them and gave them a big ice cream. It didn't matter whether it was warm sunshine or bleak and snowy, Jimmy just knew that he would come back here to live one day.

As Jimmy and Emily were waiting for their ice creams, the shop owner spotted a familiar figure as he came through the door.

"James! Look who's here!" she beamed at the doctor, who had only intended a quick visit. She pointed at the twins. "Look at them now!"

James looked at the boy and girl now looking at him with interest, then he looked at their parents behind them, who were now grinning at him. The penny then dropped!

"It's lovely to see you again, James!" from Amy. "I'm pleased to say we don't need your services today!"

James's grin now matched theirs.

"What services does James give?" Jimmy wanted to know.

James smiled at Jimmy, who was looking at him with curiosity.

I'm the local Doctor. I helped to bring you both into the world when you were born. You have grown a lot since then."

"Are you busy?" Jimmy wanted to know.

"I am!" James replied. He looked at his watch, he really needed to be at his next appointment.

"When I grow up, I will come and help you!" Jimmy said gravely.

James looked at the earnest expression on the young boy's face. He put his hand in Jimmy's.

"I will look forward to it." James said just at gravely.

"That's a deal!" Jimmy said with delight.

"Deal!" James replied with a grin, before moving to collect the item he came for and departed.

As James drove to the next patient on his home visiting round, he thought about Jimmy's words with a smile. Even if Jimmy did come to assist, he wouldn't be ready to help for another twenty years. James would probably be ready to retire by then.

James seldom had time off, as it was difficult to find a replacement. Not that he minded. James loved the wild beauty of the surrounding mountains. Their steep slopes below the snowline covered in forest. Every day, his routine was different. If his surgery and home visiting list was light, he enjoyed walking among the local walking trails. He often was called out to attend to visitors who had a mishap while climbing or skiing. There also were the car accidents of travellers, not used to the challenging road over the pass. The road had much improved in recent years, but the icy bends in winter months still caught some drivers out.

Back in the car after their ice creams, Emily was

playing with the doll she had brought with her. Jimmy sat looking out of the window, thinking of Doctor James.

Terry often took Jimmy out to the nursery with him, encouraging Jimmy to plant some seedlings and get to know all the different plants. It hadn't been spoken about, but Terry wanted Jimmy to take over the nursery when he retired.

After their return from Christchurch, Terry and Jimmy were due for a visit to the nursery. Jimmy turned to his father as they were about to leave.

"Emily should be coming too! She likes to grow plants as well."

Terry was surprised, but turned to Emily.

"Do you want to come Emily?"

"Can I?" The delight on Emily's face was plain. She jumped into the car ahead of them, her face full of excitement. At the nursery, she was full of wonder, asking lots of questions, and was reluctant to leave when it was time to go home.

"Can I come next time?" Emily wanted to know.

"Of course!" Terry smiled at her enthusiasm. Time would tell whether she maintained her interest. To Terry's surprise, it was Emily who came to work in the Nursery during the school holidays and made the cultivation of native plants her career. Amy had also encouraged Emily to learn crafts, though for Emily, they would remain a hobby to enjoy in the long winter evenings.

Once Jimmy reached High School, his future path was clear! – to achieve the highest grades he could for medical school.

The day came when Jimmy and Emily no longer accompanied their parents on their visits over the pass. Emily was looking after the nursery and Jimmy was away at university. When the Arthurs Pass shopkeeper was told where Jimmy was, she gasped with surprise.

"Well! Well! I must tell James! He will be delighted! I remember the day he told James he was coming to help him!" They all laughed at that memory.

James was updating one of his files one day when his receptionist called him.

"You have a visitor."

When James went out to the reception area, a young man, neatly dressed stood up to meet him.

"Remember me?" he said. "A while back, I said I would come to help you. Well here I am." He finished with a smile.

"Jimmy!" James said with delight. "Where are you with your training?" he asked as he led Jimmy through to his office.

"I have finished my internship at the hospitals. I am now looking for a position as a GP." Jimmy looked at James earnestly. "Coming to live and work here is my first choice, if you have room for me."

"I certainly do! Have you had any leave after your internship?" Jimmy shook his head. "No? I will send you off for a couple of weeks as it may be the last proper rest you get for a while! Once you're comfortable with managing the patients here, and familiar with the procedure for dealing with any emergencies, I will be heading off for a break myself. How does that sound?"

"It sounds great!" Jimmy was grinning as he

stood up to shake James's hand. "You can expect me in a couple of weeks."

"Have you anywhere special you will be going?" James wanted to know.

"We have a bach at Lake Kaniere I will be staying at. There is plenty for me to do. There is swimming and Kayaking on the lake, and plenty of trails to bike or walk around the lake, not to mention there is a nice climb up Mount Tuhua there too."

"I'm envious!" James said. "I wouldn't mind a holiday like that."

"Well, I could have a word with Mum and see if our bach is free when you are ready for a break."

"Deal?" James asked.

"Deal!" Jimmy replied shaking his hand again.

Jimmy had one more thing to do before he headed to the West Coast. He stopped at the shop for an ice cream. At first the shopkeeper didn't recognise Jimmy, thinking he was a businessman. After paying for it, Jimmy made the comment.

"Thank you! I thought it was about time I started paying for these!" He looked at her with a twinkle in his eyes.

The shopkeeper took a second look at the smart young man before her, and gasped. "Jimmy!"

"Yes, it's me! In a fortnight I will be back to stay. Speaking of which, are there any places to rent here? or do I bring my own tent?"

"Really?" She couldn't help laughing at the thought of him living in a tent. "There are a couple of places that are available to rent or buy if you were interested. I can call Phil down if you want a look?"

"Yes please!"

After Jimmy left, James rang his wife Maureen.

"Remember my wish to cut back to part time? Well, it is going to happen at last and in a few months we have a chance to get away for a couple of weeks to a bach on the West Coast."

When Jimmy was welcomed back into his parents' home for the night, they were both surprised and delighted, that he not only had a job lined up at Arthurs Pass, but he had organised his new home too.

KORU'S VISIT TO OKARITO

As Koru made her way to the school cave, she was aware she was being followed. Her family had spent another month at the lake community, while her father had coached her in everything he knew about the kingdom. They had now gone home to the upper Arahura Valley.

Koa had encouraged Koru to travel in the Kingdom, before she settled to having her family. He told her of Kohana's reign where her commitments to raising her family kept her away from most of her communities, relying on Koa to do the travelling for her.

Koru swiftly hid behind a tree, waiting for the footsteps to pass by. It was Koron and Kiro who had made it clear they were interested in her. As soon as they had passed, she headed in the opposite direction, nearly banging into Kerwin.

"What's up Koru? You look like you are in a hurry!"

"Don't announce it, but I am heading off." Koru said as she looked over her shoulder. "Dad has sent me to visit other communities in the kingdom, before I get busy with my own family."

"You are being pursued?"

"Yes. the visit won't happen if they catch up with me."

"Take care." Kerwin said as she moved off to disappear among the king ferns.

When Kerwin entered the cave to conduct the lessons, Koron and Kiro stood up.

"Have you seen Koru?"

"I have. She is fine. She is absent on Kingdom business. You will have to wait for her."

"How long will that be?"

"As long as it takes." Kerwin replied. 'If you can't wait, I suggest you find another mate." He saw the males look at each other. "I wouldn't try following her, if I was you," Kerwin suggested. "Koru needs to do this before she starts a family."

"So there isn't anyone else with her?"

"No. She has chosen to go alone."

Koru wasn't completely alone. As she made her way through the forest towards the south, she was being shadowed. Before Koa left, he had spoken to Oriel about Koru's trip. He had sent his daughter Omera to be her guardian.

In the days after her family returned home, Koru became aware of Omera's presence wherever she went.

"Did you want to talk to me about something? Koru asked.

Omera smiled. "I have been appointed your guardian, for when you start your journey, so I will be close by."

"Thank you!" Koru was happy she wasn't to be completely alone on her quest. "Kohana had one too, didn't she?"

"Yes, Odessa at Mahinapua was her guardian.

Koru waited till she had crossed a stream south of the settlement at Hans Bay before she stopped.

"Is anyone following us?" she asked Omera.

"No. We are alone. How far do you want to travel

Tonight?

"We will see how far we can get before first light. I will be feeding as I go. Feel free to go off for a feed. Just call me when you come back."

When daylight came, heavy clouds promised a wet day to come. Koru found a sheltered spot beneath a tree, in thick forest near the Styx River. The tree canopy gave good shelter to Omera too.

That evening, rain was still beating down. Koru dashed out for a quick forage, before returning to her temporary burrow. Taking her lead, Omera also foraged, returning with a couple of mice to keep hunger at bay for some hours.

When the rain slowed to showers, they continued on through the open farmland of Kokatahi and Kowhitirangi, crossing the swing bridge at the Gorge. Its turquoise colour waters now a muddy grey from the flood.

Several nights later, after crossing numerous streams, they came to a larger river, which was too deep and swift for Koru to cross. Heading downstream to find a bridge, Koru saw the sign "Whataroa River." She crossed the river, but continued on to the mouth of the river before heading into the forest at Okarito. Koru knew that the Okarito community lived here.

Heading towards the lagoon, Koru could hear Kiwi voices, so she made a call.

"Who is that?" a voice very near called back.

"I'm Koru. Koa sent me."

"Kahill!" the voice called out loudly. The ferns parted to reveal a male Rowi, his dark brown feathers much longer than her own. "Follow me!" he ordered her.

Koru made as much noise as she could, in the dense cover of the forest floor.

"Are you always this noisy?" the kiwi wanted to know.

"I'm just letting Omera know where I am." Koru replied serenely.

"Omera?"

"My guardian." Koru smiled, pointing at the owl sitting in the tree above, watching them intently.

"You're a long way from home!" another voice came from behind her. Koru turned around to find Kahill's twinkling eyes smiling at her.

"Kahill?" Koru asked. "Koa sent me to see how our communities are getting on."

"How is he?" Kahill asked, realising he was talking to the next Kingdom leader.

"He is well. The family are back at Arahura Valley after welcoming Kamoku and Kerwin's community to the community at Kaniere.

"Where are Kamoku and Kerwin from?" Kahill wanted to know. Their names sounded familiar.

"Kamoku is Keoni's great nephew. His father Kanoa was leader of Paparoa Community, but Kamoku has been forced out, so he has moved to the family home at Kaniere. Kerwin is Koa's friend. He was leader of Tasman community. When Kerwin found he was under threat, he left, but most of the community decided to leave with him. They are all settling in well at Kaniere."

"Have you heard how the communities at the Buller and Three sisters are going?" Kahill wanted to know.

"Kerwin and his community visited the Buller community very briefly, on their way south, but they weren't welcome, so they moved on. Kerwin did say that Kailan's widow Kari is now sharing the leadership with Kerewa."

Kahill was shocked. "What happened to Kailan?"

Kerewa's son Kahine didn't want to share the leadership with anyone, forced Kotare and Kelia out. They are at Three Sisters community. He then forced Kailan's son Kita and his friends out. They went to the Tasman, but found they were in danger there. They are now at Arthurs Pass. Kahine was expelled from the Buller. He was heading to Three Sisters to eliminate Kotare, but Kailan followed him. They had a fight and both of them died from their injuries."

Kahill shook his head at the loss of Kerewa's friend and support.

"Three Sisters Community are doing well. Kuaka gave Kamoku protection from the Paparoa community. They apparently wanted to eliminate him. When Kamoku's future mate Kirwina needed to escape from Paparoa too, she headed for Kaniere, so he escorted Kerwin and his community to Kaniere, to join her." Koru then changed the subject.

"How is your community getting on here?"

Kahill was able to smile. "It's much more peaceful here! The egg taking by the humans is helping to keep our numbers up." Some of the females grumble that they hatch more than one egg clutch a season, but at least we know that some of the eggs will grow up healthy

136

and be returned to us when they are able to defend itself." Just then a couple of young kiwis came running and crashed through between them. Kahill grinned as they passed. "That is two of them, that were raised the first year with humans."

A scandalised female voice interrupted Kahill.

"What are you doing, Kahill? Bring Koru to the burrow! She will be starving and no doubt need a rest!"

Koru turned around. A large brown feathered female Rowi, Kiori was standing there, looking at her with concern. It wasn't usual for young females to be travelling so far from home alone. Word had been sent, that Koa's daughter Koru was coming.

"Thank you!" Koru expressed her gratitude, smiling at the older female.

"You are completely alone?" Kiori was unhappy that Koa had sent her without a companion.

"Not quite." Koru looked up at the ruru sitting silently above her. "Omera is my guardian on this trip."

"Omera, you are free now till tomorrow evening."

As the Ruru silently left to feed, Kiori expressed her surprise. "You are moving on so quickly?"

"Autumn is coming soon. I want to make my trip south and return before the winter comes."

Kiori nodded at the wisdom of this. "Make sure you visit on your return."

"Thank you. I will!" Koru allowed Kiori to show her the best feeding spots and had a chat with her about the conditions here for raising their chicks.

"We would lose most of our chicks if we didn't have the eggs hatched by the humans."

"Is it like this down in Fiordland?" Koru wanted to know.

"It's worse!" Kiori replied, shaking her head. "I remember Koa and Kewena were going to have Kehi at Fiordland, but she was so unhappy at conditions down there, she insisted on coming up here! – arrived just in time to hatch her egg."

When Koru settled in Kedar's old burrow for the day, she realised that wet conditions were the biggest enemy of the communities down here. But what to do? During the day, while she was sleeping, some heavy showers came through. Koru woke to find she was wet with water flooding in on the floor. If this was what the local kiwis had to contend with, no-wonder they had trouble with hatching their chicks! Koru dug out part of the wall to make a small platform, so she had a dry area to lie on. She woke that evening to find Kahill and Kiori standing next to her. Both were damp with wet feathers. They were examining the dry area she had made for herself.

"That's a good idea!" Kahill commented. "Why didn't we think of that!"

When Koru emerged out into the forest, Omera was waiting for her.

"We will let them know you're coming." Kahill said, after their goodbyes had been said."

"Make sure you come back for another visit." Kiori reminded Koru.

"I will." Koru promised.

As they made their way south, Koru noticed that other owls and some Kereru were also following their progress. She also noticed that conditions were both cooler and wetter, the further south they travelled. One benefit, was that feeding was much easier down here.

MEETING ELI

Once they crossed the long bridge over the Haast River, Koru knew they needed to head inland. She wasn't sure just how far they needed to travel, before moving south again. Koru needn't have worried. As they followed the road, Koru heard Omera answer a Ruru's call.

"We need to go this way." Omera told her.

Several nights later as Koru steadily made her way through the dense forest, she heard a kiwi call to her.

"Is that Koru?"

"It is!" She called back. "Who is there?"

"It's Kelan."

Koru started to move towards his voice, when she found herself surrounded by local kiwis. She noticed some Ruru also came to sit in the trees around her.

"She's here!" one of them called. The kiwis parted when Kelan came. Koru noticed that all the kiwis had much longer and thicker coats than the Rowi at Okarito.

"Welcome to Fiordland." Kelan smiled as he led her to the community burrows. "The local Ruru will take care of Omera during your stay. How long will you be staying with us?"

Koru smiled. "I certainly intend to return before the Winter arrives.

"I don't blame you!" Kelan looked at Koru's dense but short grey feathers. He wasn't sure she would manage in their winter snow or wet conditions. Kelan showed Koru her burrow, before taking her to the school. Ogden was just finishing the session. Koru was amused to see that a family of Kakas were being very vocal. Koa had told her about the Kaka who dominated the classes here.

Kelan introduced Koru to the animals, who looked at her with curiosity. She was just like Koa, the other Grey kiwi that had visited them some years ago. He had become the Kingdom leader. Was this female to be the next kingdom leader? They looked behind her, there didn't seem to be a male with her.

Koru looked at the books that were lying around. They had plastic covers, which seemed to be protecting them well.

"Is there anything you need for the school?" Koru asked Ogden.

"Maybe some more slates and chalk. More books are always welcome. How will you get them to us though? Teeny Tahr has gone to the spirit world now."

"You don't have any friends among the other Tahr who will help you?" Koru asked.

"Most of them don't come down this way. They prefer to stay in the Alps."

"I will have to see what I can do." Koru commented, "Though I won't make any promises."

Ogden nodded. He understood the challenge Koru faced, bringing supplies to them. He would never forget the car journey he made with Amy and Terry to Haast Pass, then the journey with Teeny Tahr who carried all the books on a harness on his back, through the wilderness to the cave for them.

During the night, Koru told Kelan about the changes in the kingdom. When she retreated to her

141

burrow, Koru made another platform to lie on, gathering extra moss and ferns to cover it.

She was glad of it during the next couple of days and nights when constant heavy rain made the rest of her burrow very soggy. Koru made quick trips out into the rain to forage before returning to her ledge.

On the second evening as the rain eased, one of the females came to see how Koru was managing in the wet. She was astonished to see Koru was still snoozing, and completely dry.

"Who taught you to make one of those?" The kiwi asked, with wonder.

"No-one." Koru smiled at her. "I got soaked in the burrow I stayed in at Okarito, so made one of these so I could get some sleep."

The kiwi was thoughtful. "It would be handy for laying our eggs too! We lose so many from being in the wet."

Koru explored the area, finding the waterfall that Kupe's son Kamaka had jumped into, when he visited. She had no intention of jumping in – it was still in flood after the rain. The river flowing from it was a raging torrent. She hadn't expected to meet the eels on this visit, but a couple of nights later Koru was feeding by the river's edge, when she detected movement behind her. She turned around to find a large female eel had wriggled out and was coming to her.

"Is that Koa?" the eel asked in amazement.

"No. I'm his daughter, Koru."

"You look very like him! Eli will be pleased you are here to visit."

"You have a family?" the female wanted to know.

"Not yet. I won't be able to travel much once I have children. Koa told me to visit our communities now before I get busy with Kingdom duties."

"You are the Kingdom leader?"

"Not yet, but I will be."

"Make sure you come down to the river again. Eli will want to talk to you."

"I will look forward to it." Koru promised.

The female turned to the water, but then she turned back. "You are very lucky!" The female said wistfully.

"In what way?" Koru was puzzled.

"You get to know your family. We have to pass to the spirit world before we get to know ours."

"I'm sorry!" Koru spoke in sympathy. "Did the adults care for you well when you were growing up from an Elva?"

The eel though for a moment. "Not really. It was the survival of the fittest."

"You may not be able to care for your own family, but you can care for the Elva who come into your community and teach them to care for those who come after them. That way you will know that your Elva will be cared for too."

"Very wise! If I may say so!" The voice came from behind Koru. "You will make a good leader when it is your time."

Koru turned around. She hadn't noticed the other eels who had wriggled out of the water to hear the conversation.

"Hello, are you Eli?"

"I am. Where is Koa?"

"He is with his community at Arahura. He told me to visit the communities before I have my own family."

"He has taught you well. Are you coming for a ride in the river with us?"

Koru looked at the water doubtfully, it still looked swollen from the rain.

"We will make sure you don't fall in and we will bring you back." the female added persuasively. "Sit on my back and hold on tight!"

When Koru gingerly stood on the female's back, she nearly fell off again, so another female wriggled beside her, for Koru to stand on her back too. Gently they lowered themselves back into the water together, before moving out into the middle of the river, with all the other eels swimming alongside them. Koru gasped as the cold water washed over her claws, but was also exhilarated as she was swept downstream.

As Koru enjoyed the view of the forest from the eels' backs, she was surprised to see some kiwis on the river bank. She now recognised all the kiwis in Kelan's community. These were a separate community. She saw they were as amazed to see her, as she was of them.

Koru nodded her head and smiled as she passed them. A few miles downstream, her feet were becoming cold and she wasn't sure she would be able to hold on for too long.

"Can we go back now? My feet are getting cold!

Silently and smoothly the eels turned around to

144

return to Kelan's community. The strange Kiwis were still on the bank as Koru returned. Some more kiwis had joined them.

"Hello!" Koru called out to them, as they came into view. "I am Koru."

"Where are you from?" a kiwi called from the bank.

"I am from Kaniere in the north. I am staying with Kelan's community."

As Koru disappeared round the next bend, the kiwis were also amazed that this kiwi, a different species from them, not only had a relationship with the eels, that they allowed her to stand on their backs, but she also came from a place that had a name. How did she know it had a name? Also how did she get to know Kelan's community? There were so many questions they would have liked to ask her.

This group of kiwis knew of Kelan's community, but in the interests of harmony, had kept completely separate. They had made the mistake of having encounters with the group, when Kona was in charge, suffering the loss of two of their members. If Kelan's group could have a good relationship with other species, perhaps it was now safe to have a relationship with them?

When the eels deposited Koru on the bank, she ended up sitting down, as her feet were now numb. She didn't mind though. The experience was something she would remember and cherish for the rest of her life.

"Thank you!" Koru called to the eels as they returned to the water. "That was wonderful."

The sound of movement in the bushes behind her, heralded the arrival of Kelan and some of the community.

"There you are! We wondered where you had got to!"

Koru smiled. "I was just having a ride down the river with the eels! Did you know there is another group of kiwis here?"

Kelan's eyes were sad as he nodded. "They had contact with our community during Dad's time, but he killed two of them. They have kept well away from us ever since. You didn't speak to them at all?"

"I did! I said Hello, telling them my name. They wanted to know where I was from, so I told them and that I was visiting your community. You may find them more approachable now."

"How far away are they?" Kelan wanted to know. "Can you show me where you saw them?"

Koru went to stand up, found herself hobbling, as the feeling was still returning to her feet. "My feet were cold in the water." She explained.

Kelan understood. In Winter time when snow was on the ground for long periods, they also had problems with walking when their feet became very cold.

They made their way along the bank untill they heard the voices of the kiwis from the other community. Koru called out to them.

"Hello! It's Koru."

Some of the Kiwis appeared on the other side of the river. "I have Kelan with me."

"Hello!" Kelan called out. "I want to say sorry for

146

what Kona did when your community last met ours."

"Is he still around?"

"No. He has gone to the spirit world now."

"Nice to meet you Koru and Kelan." The kiwis then disappeared into the forest.

"Well, it's a start, thank you Koru."

A couple of nights later, frost developed on the ground, making it harder to feed.

"It's time I went back." Koru mentioned to Kelan, before she settled to sleep. "We will leave this evening."

"We will miss you!" Kelan said. "Make sure you stay safe."

As Koru and Omera made their way north, Kelan and his community weren't the only ones to watch her go; - noticing that she was accompanied by an owl.

"That Koru is a very special Kiwi." The Tokoeka leader commented. "I wonder whether she will return."

When Koru and Omera reached Okarito, they both were ready for a break from travelling. The wet and blustery weather was a good excuse for a week's rest.

"You have done well!" Kahill approved, when Koru told him of the meeting she had engineered between the two communities. "It is early days, but a reconciliation between the two groups may come now."

"Where are you heading next?" Kahill wanted to know, when Koru was ready to move on.

"I will visit the northern communities, starting with Three Sisters Community."

"Take care! The Buller is still volatile!" Kahill warned.

"I'm not expecting any trouble." Koru remained

serene. "My father was part of their community along with Kerewa when they were younger. Kerewa is still in charge, along with Kari. I am looking forward to seeing how their partnership is working."

However, with Kahill's caution in the back of her mind, Koru made the long trek up the coast.

CHANGE COMES TO THE KINGDOM

Koru made her way up the Ohikanui Valley. She had just come from a pleasant stay at Three Sisters Mountain Community.

Kuaka had sent Odion up to the Buller community, to see whether it was safe for Koru to travel there. He was able to report that the community had settled again, after the visit by Kerwin's community and that Kerewa and Katana were looking forward to seeing her.

Some of the kiwis at Kaniere had mentioned, they lived in this valley before they moved to the lake; but the flooding had forced them to move on. Koru made sure she made her burrow high on the valley slopes, just in case a flood swept through while she was sleeping. Koru noticed that Omera was having more contact than usual with the local owls as they moved up the valley.

"Is everything alright?" Koru asked.

"Everything is fine." Omera reassured her. "They were interested to see the next Kiwi Kingdom leader. They haven't seen one since Kohana came through, when she was the kingdom leader. Also, they were interested to hear about our travels down to Fiordland and Okarito."

At the Buller community, Kari's chick, Kaitoa, liked to hear about his father, but she encouraged him to be completely independent. There was some pressure for her to choose another mate, but she was taking her time, deciding whether she would breed again or not.

Being a leader and making sure all the females were well taken care of, took a great deal of her time. Kari was fully aware that if she took another mate, that he would want some influence on the leadership. She was now asking herself whether she could trust any of the males to respect her position and not use their relationship for their own leadership ambitions. There was also the matter of Kaitoa's safety if she had other children.

When Kerewa mentioned to Kari that his niece Koru was coming for a visit, she looked at him enquiringly.

"She is Koa's daughter, isn't she? Has he sent her here on Kingdom business, or is she here for a family visit?"

"To be honest, I don't know the exact reason for her visit." Kerewa felt uncomfortable as he spoke.

"Kuaka at Three Sisters Community sent one of their owls up while Koru was visiting them, to see if it was safe for her to visit. I sent word back the community was settled again after Kerwin's visit and that Katana and I were looking forward to seeing her."

The anger now in Kari's face told Kerewa that he had made a mistake.

"I'm sorry." Kerewa apologised.

"This is supposed to be a joint partnership! No - one comes here without us both knowing why they are coming! Where is she now? And who is coming with her?"

"Koru is on her way here through the Ohikanui. She has a Ruru, Omera with her."

"Send Oren and ask her whether her visit is for Kingdom or family business. She is to wait for approval to come here."

Kerewa called for Oren. Opal appeared.

"You want help with something?"

"Can either you or Oren go to the Ohikanui and find Koru and Omera who are on their way here."

Opal nodded. "We had heard they are coming."

"Tell Koru we need to know whether her visit is for Kingdom business or family visit. They are to wait in the Ohikanui for permission to visit."

By the serious expression on Kerewa's face, she knew that something was wrong. Opal swiftly flew towards the Ohikanui valley. She knew they weren't far away.

To Opal's dismay, she could see a kiwi swimming the river towards the community, a Ruru was hovering over her. It could only be Koru and Omera. On the community side of the river some members of the community were waiting with grim looks on their faces.

Opal landed in front of the waiting kiwis and spoke to them.

"Please welcome this kiwi and bring her to Kerewa and Kari. She is Koru, the daughter of Koa, Kerewa's brother who used to live her. Kerewa and Katana are expecting her.

Opal was relieved to see the grim expressions change to smiles at Koa's name. As Koru emerged from the water, Opal called to Omera.

"I will go ahead to let them know you are here."

Koru was relieved to see a Ruru land and tell the

waiting kiwis who she was. Their expressions had been grim and not at all welcoming, before the Ruru intervened. It seemed that the situation here, was still volatile when it came to strangers.

"Welcome Koru! Who is your owl?" they wanted to know.

"Thank you!" Koru smiled back at them. "Please meet Omera."

"Please come with us. We will find Kerewa for you. How is Koa?" One of the kiwis asked, as they walked.

"Koa is well. He is too busy to visit the communities now, so he sent me to visit all the communities to make sure everyone is managing well."

The kiwis were looking at her quizzically. "You don't have any brothers to go on such a long trip?"

"I do, but they haven't been chosen to be the next Kingdom Leader. Koa asked me to come, before I get busy with raising a family."

"There was silence for a few seconds as the Kiwis digested what Koru had revealed to them."

"It is our honour to have you with us! Did you know that Kohana was based here? Do Kerewa and Kari know?'

"Not yet! Yes Koa told me about Kohana and Kehi's life here. Koru smiled at them.

"While you are here, we will be your bodyguard."

"Thank you!"

"Kerewa? Kari?" Opal called out as she approached the spot where she last saw them.

"You found her?" Kerewa asked "Where is she?"

"Did you find out why she is here?" Kari's tone was tense.

During the time they waited for Opal's return, Kari had made up her mind! Kerewa and his family had to go! She already knew which of the males vying to mate with her she would choose. Kaitoa, her son by Kailan was being encouraged to be completely independent of her. There would be no prospect of him being a leader. Her children by her new partner would be the future leaders.

"Koru was already crossing the river when I found her. She is receiving an escort to you now."

"Whatever the reason Koru is here, she won't be staying!" Kari's words were final. Her next words make Kerewa's blood run cold. "It's time to sort the leadership too!" She then made a loud call, for everyone to go to the meeting area.

"Where are you going?" Kari's tone was sharp as Kerewa turned to leave her.

"It is obvious you intend to replace me as leader. As of now, you no longer control me! I am going to find my family."

Kerewa brushed past kiwis who had witnessed the exchange, calling out for Katana and Kiyo, their daughter. She was named after his mother. As Kerewa ran towards his burrow, he came across the Kiwis giving Koru an escort.

"Hello Koru! I'm sorry, but it isn't safe for you to be here. You need to return across the river."

"We are being her body guards." One of the Kiwis spoke. "We will take her to the bridge."

"Thank you. Make sure she is safely on the other side. Koru I expect to join you shortly, if I'm not killed."

"What's going on?"

"Kari is taking over the leadership."

The kiwis looked at each other. 'We've been down this road before!" Two of the Kiwis came to stay with Kerewa. The others swiftly lead Koru away.

"Katana!" Kerewa called again.

"I'm here! Aren't you going to the meeting?" She had Kiyo and Kaitoa with her.

"I am, but you need to leave now, just in case I don't make it." Kerewa nodded at the look of alarm on Katana's face. "I am being replaced as leader. Go to the other side of the bridge." Katana tried to protest. "GO!"

Kerewa grimly made his way to the meeting area. He was glad he wasn't completely alone. When he arrived, everyone was already here before him. He knew that rumours were already flying among the crowd. Instead of joining Kari out in the middle as he usually did, Kerewa stayed on the edge, ready to flee if he needed to.

"Why aren't you joining me?" Kari called to Kerewa. And, where is Koru and your family?"

"You called this meeting. You have the floor." Kerewa answered in a neutral tone, staying where he was. He didn't answer her question about Koru and the family.

Kari had the feeling that Kerewa had outmanoeuvred her! Her anger now showed.

"Where is Koru? Why is she here?" Kari demanded.

154

"You won't be finding out. She has already left the community, after I made it clear she isn't safe here."

"Who is Koru?" a kiwi in the audience called out.

"Koru is my brother Koa's daughter."

"Why isn't she safe here?" came another call. Kerewa didn't answer, but pointedly looked at Kari.

"Kari, you told me that you were going to sort the leadership."

The crowd fell silent at this news.

A look of triumph came to Kari's face.

"I am going to choose my next mate. They will lead the community with me."

Before anyone could stop him, Kerewa turned on his heel and began running for his life! The two males ran with him. On seeing this, their mates and children also stood up to leave. Several other families also withdrew from the area. They guessed Kerewa and his family went to the bridge and headed that way too.

The kiwis took Koru across the bridge and waited. Soon a large female with two young kiwis came running to the bridge, checking behind them before crossing to join Koru.

"I'm Katana, Kerewa's mate. This is our daughter Kiyo and Kari's son Kaitoa, by Kailan." She turned to the young male at Kiyo's side. "Are you sure you don't want to stay with your mother?"

"No." Kaitoa's tone was full of hurt. "She doesn't want me around her now." Katana gave him a cuddle.

"You can be part of our family now if you want."

The sound of more footsteps could be heard. Katana was relieved to see Kerewa and two kiwis with him cross the bridge. By the time everyone reached the Ohikanui Valley, they found other families already waiting for them, having made the dangerous crossing over the river, after their access to the bridge was cut off.

They had stories of clashes between supporters of Kerewa and the supporters of the new leaders.

"What are you going to do Kerewa?" Koru asked, when everyone had found a spot to sleep for the morning.

"It occurred to me some time ago that one day I might have to make a quick exit from here, so I had look at the atlas to see if there was anywhere suitable to set up another home." Kerewa smiled. "I will visit Kuaka to see Kotare and Kelia, then will head to the Arahura Valley. I will join Koa's community. It is close to both the Arthur's Pass and Kaniere communities."

When Kerewa and his kiwis woke that evening, they found out why Kerwin and his community didn't stay here. There had been heavy rain during the day. Now the river levels were up high. Small waterfalls cascaded down the steep slopes of the valley.

Venturing out only for a feed, they stayed in their burrows till the weather cleared.

When word came that Kerewa and some of his community were near Three Sisters community, Kuaka, Koro, Kotare and Kelia came down the mountain to meet them and the new arrivals.

"I have something for you to take back." Kelia said to Koru. She hooked her claw through the amulet around her neck, pulling it over her head and passed it to Koru, who pulled it over her head.

On learning of the developments in the Buller, Kuaka made the comment.

"It's the end of an era. It will be interesting to see how the Buller community manage under their new leaders."

In the Buller, Kari was finding that she had made a mistake with her choice, but her pride didn't allow her to admit it to anyone. Her new partner ruled over both her and the community with a ruthlessness she hadn't expected. Her expectation of continuing to help the females dissolved – she was now too busy looking after the survival of both herself and her egg.

One night, a female confronted Kari.

"Are you happy?" Kari swiftly looked around, keeping a neutral expression, before looking back at her. Kari's silence told her everything she needed to know.

Kerewa followed Kerwin's path untill they came to the Arahura river, turning inland to follow the river upstream. As he passed the steep slopes of Mount Tuhua, Kerewa was tempted to call in at the Lake Kaniere community, but he resisted. There was plenty of time later to catch up with Kerwin. Everyone had had enough of travelling now, and just wanted to settle somewhere safe.

Koru also was tempted to deviate to the lake, but she needed to make sure Kerewa's community were settled. She also needed to visit Koen to make sure all was well up in Arthurs Pass.

When Koru and Kerewa's community arrived, all was quiet. A crowd was gathered around Koa, who was lying on the ground. It was obvious that Koa had been badly injured.

"Dad! What happened?" Koru asked as she pushed her way through the crowd, with Kerewa at her heels.

"He fell!" Kewena his mate, was sitting next to him. Her voice was full of anguish. She hadn't expected to find happiness a second time, but now he too was leaving her.

Koa opened his eyes. Focusing first on Koru.

"So you made it back home." He greeted her.

He then looked at Kerewa. "Look after them all for me." Before closing his eyes for the last time.

Koru looked up at Omera, who was watching from the tree above. "Can you tell Oriel?"

Oriel was taking the class in the cave, when Omera flew in. He expected Koru to come running down the steps behind her, but Omera was alone.

"Koru is at the Arahura community. Kerewa and some of his community are there too. Koa had a fall. He has just moved to the spirit world."

"Tell her to take her time, and make sure they all are settled over there. We will expect her home then."

Orion had seen Omera back in the forest, came to see the latest news. Omera was flying out as he came in to the cave.

"Can you spread the word to the other leaders," Oriel told Orion. "The Kingdom has a new leader."

When Omera returned to the Arahura Valley community, Koru was introducing the new families to the community, who were showing them where to make their new burrows and the feeding areas.

"I have one more job for you." Koru said to Omera

as she took two amulets from around her neck and placed them over Omera's head. The amulet Koa had worn now joined the amulet Kelia had given Koru. "Can you give these to Oriel to place in the book?"

When Kerwin came down from Mount Tuhua after giving Oregon his lessons, he came into the school cave to find Oriel with the Kiwi Kingdom book open, and the amulets in his claw.

"What's happening?"

"Koa has just passed to the spirit world. The amulets are being returned to the book untill the new leader is ready to begin her duties." He smiled at Kerwin. She brought Kerewa and some of his community to Arahura. Koa asked Kerewa to be the leader there."

"Who is leading at Buller now?"

"Kailan's widow Kari has taken another mate. Kerewa and his supporters had to flee for their lives. Whether Kari and her mate stay in the kingdom, time will tell."

At the Buller, all the books had been moved to another cave, well away from the kiwi community. The glow worms had moved too. The first evening after Kerewa's departure, a kiwi came and tried to destroy the books. The Possums had to threaten him before he withdrew. When he returned with reinforcements, the animals had removed the books from the area.

At the Arahura Valley, the new arrivals were missing their classes. Koru promised to organise some book and slates for them.

THE NEW LEADER

When Koru returned to her community at Lake Kaniere, Koen from Arthurs Pass community came with her. His excuse was that he wanted to visit Oriel.

Kerewa would have liked to come with them, for a visit to the lake, but that would have to wait for another time. Both the local community and his own families were more settled than he had expected. It helped a great deal that Kerewa was Koa's brother and that Koa had asked him to be leader here.

Their sister Kiana had been comforting Kewena after her loss, was now with Koru and Koen for a break; leaving her chick with her mate. Kewena was also expecting Koa's legacy, so she would be needing some help to hatch her chick when the time came.

There was excitement among the birds as they came to Mount Tuhua. Koru didn't take too much notice, till they came to climb down into the school cave. It was full of animals, waiting for them to arrive. Among them were Kelan and Kahill from Fiordland and Okarito and Kuaka from Three Sisters Community. Omera was sitting with the Ruru family. Oriel was waiting at the front with the Kiwi Kingdom Book open.

As Koru took her vows to serve the Kingdom, there were two nervous kiwis among the crowd who were wondering whether she would still be interested in them, now that she was leader of the kingdom. They could see that Koru had matured a great deal during her time away.

160

After the ceremony, Oriel wanted to know what her first mission was.

"We need some books and slates for the Arahura community. The families who came with Kerewa are missing their lessons."

"We will take you to see Amy."

One evening when Amy and Lucy's family were at the bach, Koru was led through the garden to the shed by Kerwin, while Oriel waited in the tree above. Koru would have liked to explore the garden some more, after feeling all the worms underfoot.

After Kerwin had led Koru up the stairs, Oriel flew in to stand between them. He scratched at the door. For once no-one had spotted them come, so there was a scramble by both Amy and Lucy to collect items as Hoani and Terry brought the children to the window.

"Oh! There are three of them!" Naku said excitedly as he peered through the window.

Koru was nervous at being so close to humans, but she allowed herself to be led by Oriel and Kerwin who had been here before.

"Hello Oriel. Hello Kerwin!" Amy said as she opened the door. "And who is this you have brought with you?"

Amy could see straight away that this was an adult female Kiwi they had brought with them. She had a jade pendant around her neck too! She obviously was a leader. Amy smiled at the new kiwi as she kneeled on the floor and brought out a slate, chalk and the atlas.

'Do you want more books?' Amy wrote on the slate.

Oriel brought Koru forward to see the words on the slate. She immediately grabbed the chalk and wrote 'Yes Arahura Valley '

On seeing the 'Yes' Amy brought out the atlas. Koru recognised what the atlas was and came forward to look with Oriel and Kerwin.

"We are here." Amy tapped the lake with her finger. She then traced the Arahura River valley with her finger, to its source. She then wrote on the slate.

'Where do you want your books?'

Koru pointed to a spot on the map. Amy put her finger on the spot. "Lucy can you get me a pen?"

Koru backed off a little when this other human came to the door to give Amy the pen. Amy then marked the spot with an X.

'We will bring books. What is her name?'

"She wants to know your name." Kerwin told Koru.

Koru grabbed the chalk and wrote KORU.

Amy pointed at her name on the slate and spoke "Koru." Before pointing at Koru and said her name. Amy then wrote on the slate.

'Is Koru your leader?'

Kerwin grabbed the chalk to reply 'Yes Kingdom leader.'

"They will bring the books when they are ready, so we can go now."

As Koru turned to follow Oriel and Kerwin off the veranda she spotted all the other humans watching them from behind the window. They had a dog with them too! She didn't linger, but swiftly followed Kerwin into the garden.

"Are you sure it's safe to stay?" Koru asked Kerwin when he stopped to feed in the garden. His answer was to call to Karamu and the children to join them. Koru noticed that Kerwin and his family ignored the human family when they came out onto the veranda to watch them feed.

"It's quite safe in this garden." Kerwin reassured her. "Cats are quite easy to chase away. It is only the dogs we have to be careful of. Most of them are kept on leads now."

"Hello Hovea!" Kerwin called when the Hedgehog came out from under the bach to join them, to feed in the garden.

"Hello" Hovea called back. She spotted the amulet that Koru was wearing.

"Are you the Kingdom leader now?" Hovea asked as she came over to Koru.

"I am." Koru smiled back at her.

"Welcome home to your kingdom."

As Koru fed, she found herself thinking about the two males who were competing to be her mate. She realised there was a question she needed to ask them before she made her decision.

When Koru returned to the community, Koron and Kiro were waiting for her.

"Come with me." Koru bade them, a neutral expression on her face.

Up to the top of Mount Tuhua, she led them. She was pleased there was a full moon, so she could see their expressions easily. Koru told them to stand together, their faces plain to see.

"I have a question to ask you." Koru began. Kiro was going to ask why she couldn't ask it down in the community, but thought better of it; realising that they were being put to a test. So he stayed silent and waited for Koru to speak.

"There will be times when my Kingdom duties may have to come before my family duties. Are you able to support me with this?"

The difference in their attitudes was immediately apparent. Koron broke into a loving smile and nodded. Kiro kept his expression neutral. After a couple of seconds he replied "Of course!"

"Thank you for your interest, Kiro. You may go."

He looked at Koron, but Koron only had eyes for Koru.

"I wondered how you would solve that question. " Koron spoke as he came over to cuddle her.

"Do you approve?" Koru allowed herself to relax against him.

"I do. I know our relationship won't be a traditional one, as my main role will be to support you."

Koru gave him a radiant smile.

"We will have a good life together."

LIVING WORLD ANIMALS

Roroa Kiwis
Tasman:	-Kerwin (Leader) & Karamu
	– Kamahi, Kahuia, Karri
Buller:	-Kerewa (Joint Leader) & Katana
	- Kahine, Kiyo
	-Kari (Joint Leader)
	- Kita, Kaitoa
	-Kita's friends - Kohu, Kimo
Arthurs Pass	-Koen (Leader)
Arahura:	-Koa (Kingdom leader) & Kewena
	- Kehi, Koru
	-Kio (Keona & Keio)
Paparoa:	-Kirwina
	-Kera
Three Sisters	-Kuaka (Leader)
	-Kamoku
	-Koro, Kotare, Kelia
Lake Kaniere	-Koron, Kiro, Kena

Rowi Kiwi

Okarito:	-Kahill (Leader) & Kiori

Tokoeka Kiwi
Fiordland:	-Kelan (Leader)

Owls/Ruru
Tasman:	- Oreana & Oren
	-Orok
Buller:	-Opal

LIVING WORLD ANIMALS (CONT.)

Three Sisters -Odion (leader) & Oana
Lake Kaniere- Oriel (Kingdom Guardian) & Odele
                    - Omera
            -Orion
            -Oregon (Spirit world leader) & Ophena
Fiordland: -Ocene (Leader)
            -Ogden

SPIRIT WORLD ANIMALS

Kiwis:	Keoni - First Leader of the Kiwi Kingdom
	Kupe - Keoni's great Grandson, next leader of Kingdom
	Kaori - Kupe's friend
	Kohana – Kupe's daughter, leader of kingdom after Kupe
	Kanoa - Kupe's cousin, Leader at Paparoa
	Kailan – Joint leader of Buller with Kerewa
Dog:	Titan, Kohana's companion in the spirit world
Haast Eagles:	Hirone – Leader of Nudoor
	Haina - Odelia's guardian
	Haera - Oregon's guardian
	Hiena - Ophena's guardian
	Hira
Harrier:	Hagar
Marsupial Lion:	Minjarra

Moas: Manu, Moana
Morepork Owl/Ruru: Odelia

HUMAN FAMILY

Amy (Emily's Great granddaughter) & Terry
         - Jimmy & Emily
Lucy (Amy's daughter) & Hoani
         - Alice & Naku
Reka (Hoani's sister) & Kiwa
         - Kohi & Moana
Mahina (Reka's friend) & Toro
         - Tama, Taiko, Rangi
         - Toby (Tama's friend)
Hori & Kohi - Reka and Hoani's parents
Kawa   - Mahina's brother, leader of a gang in
          Auckland
Mike (Kiwa's friend at Lake Kaniere) & Anne
         - Ash
Noah   - leader of gang in Auckland
Pua   - Noah's sister, married to Kawa.

Printed in Australia
AUHW010936140422
362328AU00018B/40